Amish

Christmas

The Bakery

Samantha Bayarr

An Amish Christmas: The Bakery

Newly Released books
99 cents or FREE with
Kindle Unlimited.

♡ LOVE to Read?
♡ LOVE 99 cent Books?
♡ LOVE GIVEAWAYS?

SIGN UP NOW
Click the Link Below to Join
my Exclusive Mailing List

PLEASE CLICK <u>HERE</u> to SIGN UP!

TABLE OF CONTENTS

CHAPTER ONE

HUNTER packed his daughter's lunch. PB&J on honey-wheat bread, check. Apple slices, check. A handful of almonds, check. A couple of Oreos strategically folded in her napkin, check!

Phooey on Mrs. Wilkins and her strict, healthy-snacks-only policy!

"Let's go, Raegan," he called to his five-year-old daughter for the umpteenth time. "We're going to be late—again!"

His daughter walked into the kitchen—pouty-faced, her hair ratted up at least three full inches off the top of her head, and she'd squirted toothpaste all down the front of her last clean uniform.

"Rae, you're doing a great job of making me look like *father of the year!*"

She smiled.

"Not funny!" he said, reaching for the kitchen towel and running it under the faucet to wet a corner of it. "Let's take care of one crisis at a time."

He wiped at the front of her uniform jumper, but it wasn't easy getting rid of the white contrast to the deep navy of the dress.

Once the toothpaste stain was cleaned from the front of her uniform, he went about the task of trying to brush out her unruly, auburn locks that reminded him too much of her mother. The woman had a plain beauty like no other woman he'd ever met. A beauty that matched her insides; it had caused his friends to envy him.

They didn't envy him now that she was gone.

In fact, they'd all-but abandoned him—or he'd pushed them all away because of his grief. He couldn't be sure which, but he suspected it was a little of both. No one wanted to be around someone who was constantly down-in-the-mouth; he certainly fit that description, but more so with the holidays fast approaching.

Hunter shook away his brief regression and concentrated on the present—his daughter, who was very much alive, and probably more in need of a mother to help with these tasks than he was willing to admit. His older sister,

Holly, had tried many times to coax him out on a blind date, but he just didn't feel the need to force such a thing.

It'll happen if it's supposed to—and in God's timing—not mine, he'd told her.

She'd accepted his answer even though she knew it was a copout. It hadn't stopped her from dropping not-so-subtle hints now and then.

"Ow!" Raegan squealed. "Brush it like Aunt Holly used to—before she left us!"

"Sweetie, she didn't leave us because she wanted to; Uncle Earl had to move to a different office with his company."

Raegan pushed out her lower lip to show her unhappiness with the situation. She hadn't meant for her comment to sting, but it did. He didn't like it anymore than she did. He'd come to depend on his sister's help since Kate's death, but the time had come for the two of them to be on their own and figure things out.

He'd had his sister as a crutch for the past two years, and it was time for him to be more independent.

Had it really been that long?

He wasn't sure if he'd ever get used to downtown living. Though he'd put the house up for sale immediately after Kate's funeral, he'd refused several offers just so he could hold on a little longer. At first, he hadn't been able to face the ghosts; every room reminded him of her, especially the yard with all the flowering plants she'd so lovingly cared for that attracted all the butterflies.

She loved butterflies.

He'd originally planned on renting out the space above his furniture shop in town, but it seemed more logical for him to move into the newly-remodeled oversized loft above the woodshop.

Hunter took a step back and observed his daughter; she was presentable and clean now.

"Can you put one of those rubber band things in your hair now the way Aunt Holly taught you?"

"Daddy; she taught you, too!"

He nodded. "You're better at it than I am." His sister had taught him a lot of the little things—most of which, he'd already forgotten. "Can you do your hair in the truck on the way there? If we don't leave now, we'll be late, and you know the ladies in car line don't like that."

"Why can't I ride with Jenna? Her mom is always telling me to ask you if she can pick me up, so you don't have to."

I'm sure she does.

Her innocent eyes saddened him. She had no idea that the woman's offer came with another unscrupulous offer for *him;* he wasn't about to owe a lonely divorcee anything!

"I'm driving you because that's *my* job to take you," he said, grabbing her backpack off the floor and weighing it in his hand. "When's the last time you emptied this thing, Squirt?"

She shrugged.

"I had no idea you were lugging this much stuff around; let's empty some of the unnecessary stuff so you can tote it around a little easier."

He flung it up on the counter and dumped the contents; it would be much easier to start over than rifling through it for things she no longer needed—especially when they were already running late.

"Look at all these papers," he said, grabbing pencils and books to put back in the pack. "Where did all this stuff come from?"

"It's notes for you, Daddy!"

"You do know you're supposed to give those to me, right?"

Raegan rolled her eyes.

Something tells me I've missed a parent-teacher conference or something!

HUNTER ducked when he saw Jenna Parker's mom walking toward his truck.

Oh, Lord, please don't let her come and talk to me!

"Mr. Darcy!" she said, fake charm dripping from her tone. "I'm so glad I caught up with you."

He clenched his jaw and turned, unable to avoid her; she was at his truck window and there were too many cars in front of him in the line for him to move out of the way.

"Mrs. Parker," he said.

She curled her lip for just a moment and then quickly replaced it with a forced smile.

"*Ms.* Parker, silly," she said with a forced giggle. "I was divorced over the summer; I know I told you that before."

More than once!

Now it was his turn to force a smile. The less he said to her, the faster he could get away from the needy woman, right?

"I really wish you'd call me Alice."

When he said nothing, she continued, her tone annoyed. "I wanted to talk to you about the class Christmas party. As class volunteer coordinator—and PTA president, I'll need to know what you're bringing so I can put it on my list. That, and I'd hate to clash with anyone."

Treats? I'm supposed to bring treats? Hmm, the unread notes in the backpack.

"I was so happy when Raegan volunteered you to bring something," she said.

Volunteered me?

"Raegan did tell you, didn't she?"

He nodded; not true, but he had a feeling if he admitted he'd been caught off guard, she'd offer to help in some way, and he didn't need her kind of *help.*

That little Squirt is grounded!

"Just remember that everything has to be homemade; if you need help with the baking, I'd be more than happy to help you."

"NO!" He pasted on a smile and chuckled nervously when he realized he'd raised his voice. "I'm making—gingerbread— cookies," he said, fumbling over his words.

Gingerbread? Couldn't I have come up with something easier than that?

"Gingerbread! That's ambitious; one more of those little things that makes you so appealing, Mr. Darcy. Now, if I could just get you to humor me and speak to me with an English accent."

She wrinkled up her nose and winked at him.

"I've got to go," he said abruptly, seeing the car in front of him had moved out of his way in line. "I've got to get to work."

She waved furiously as he drove off; he didn't look back for fear he'd turn into a pillar of salt.

CHAPTER TWO

HUNTER drove away from car-line at the elementary school, pausing for a moment before pulling out onto the street. Kate would have been so proud to have her daughter as a student. When they were first married, he'd driven her to school every morning and dropped her off in the same spot he now dropped off their daughter. After their first year of marriage, she'd become pregnant with

Raegan and had given up teaching, though she had planned to homeschool their daughter. It was days like this that made him wish more than anything that those dreams had come to pass—but they hadn't, and there was no sense in wishing for something that would not happen.

He pushed the phone button on his steering wheel, the ringing coming through his truck speakers.

"Congratulations," Holly said from the other end of the line.

"Huh?" Hunter said. "For what?"

"Because you've managed to get through an entire week without calling me because of a crisis."

"How do you figure I'm calling you because I'm having a crisis?"

Holly's laugh echoed through the cab of the truck. "Because it's eight-thirty-seven in the morning, which means you're probably just now leaving car-line after dropping off Raegan."

"You think you're so smart," he grumbled.

"If I'm wrong, I apologize."

He blew out a discouraging breath; she knew him too well. "You're not wrong."

"Tell me what happened, and let's see if we can' put our heads together and fix whatever it is."

"I don't think this one can be fixed," he grumbled. "I opened my big mouth and stuck my big foot right in!"

"You've always been good at that!"

"Not helping, Holly, I've got to make three dozen gingerbread cookies for Raegan's class Christmas party on Friday."

"Who said you had to?"

He pulled up to the light at Main Street. He hated this one; it was a long one.

"I said. Raegan volunteered me, but when that bossy Jenna Parker's mother cornered me in car-line, I told her I'd bake them."

"What did you go and do a thing like that for?" Holly asked.

He could hear the strain in her voice.

"My daughter asked if I'd let Jenna's mom take her to school," he said. "That Jenna is always bossing Raegan around, and her mother is even worse! Holly, I feel like I'm losing my daughter; if I can't bake these cookies for her, I'll fail her."

"You aren't going to fail her; you're a great dad," Holly said. "I'm sure Rae only asked because that little Jenna is putting pressure on her—and probably the mom is too. Pull yourself together; we have two days to figure this out."

"Mrs.—I mean, *Ms.* Parker offered to help me bake something, but I'm afraid she'd latch onto me and think I was her next husband, and I don't want that."

"She's had her eye on you since the school year started; isn't she the one who thinks you're her *Mr. Darcy?*"

Holly laughed.

"It isn't funny! That woman has stars in her eyes for me, and I don't like it; she's way too forward—brash. I'm not some story-book hero who's interested in playing a part in her fictitious life, and if she asks me to speak with an English accent once more, I'm going to— well, I'm going to have to be really firm with her, and you know she'll take it as being rude."

"Yeah, I'd have to say keep it on the back burner, but you might have to ask for help."

"NOT from her! I'll try it myself, first; Kate had a ton of recipes and I kept all of them in case Raegan wanted them when she was older. I'm sure I can whip something up; how hard could it be?"

"I don't know, little brother; if you show up with burnt cookies, those PTA ladies can be mean!"

"I've already noticed that; Ms. Parker is the PTA president, remember?"

"Isn't there an Amish bakery two blocks over from your shop—on the other side of the park?"

"I don't know," he said with a sigh.

"You're going to have to start getting creative if you're going to survive this parenting thing," Holly said. "It's okay to cheat this time since you're in a time-crunch, but you really need to learn how to bake—and cook more than just spaghetti and mac & cheese!"

"But those are my specialties," he said with a chuckle.

"All joking aside; how are you holding up? I know this has to be tough since this will be your first Christmas alone as a single dad— and without your big-sis to hold your hand."

He rounded the corner of Main Street and there in front of him was the very Bakery his sister had told him about; how had he never noticed it before?

"I found that bakery you were talking about."

"Go order your cookies and we'll worry about sharpening your cooking skills before the next crisis hits," Holly said.

He told her goodbye and clicked the button on his steering wheel as he pulled into a parking spot in front of *Bäckerei Noel*.

He hopped out of his truck and peered into the window; all the lights were off, but the sun streaming in through the front window showed off all sorts of cakes, cookies and pastries. The front window boasted an entire gingerbread village. Each building was iced with intricate scrollwork and the architecture was amazing. Being a carpenter, he was in awe of each little building's unique design. They were much like the Amish houses he'd seen being constructed in the area. The gingerbread *people* were mostly dressed as Amish, but some were traditionally outfitted. Fluffy, polyester *snow* covered the bottom of the display.

Wouldn't Ms. Parker's jaw drop if he showed up with such a display for the Christmas party?

He imagined such a village was certainly way out of his price range, but that didn't keep him from chuckling at the thought of her envious expression if he should walk into the classroom with that.

A gust of icy wind brought Hunter from his reverie; he walked up to the door of the bakery to see the hours on the glass. He looked at his watch; they would not open for another eight minutes. He could wait that long. Going back to his truck, he stomped the slush from his boots and then hopped in. He turned the key and flipped the heater on high, and then pushed the button for the seat warmer.

NOEL Fisher finished icing the last of the gingerbread cookies for her daily orders, and went about wiping down the stainless-steel kitchen counters, and filled the large stainless-steel sink to soak the sticky bowls and utensils so she could wash them later after her opening crowd slowed.

She tied on a clean apron and suppressed a yawn as she climbed the stairs to the small apartment above her bakery. It wasn't much, but it was paid for—after selling the farm she'd shared with her husband. She'd purchased the building from the proceeds because she just couldn't bear to live on the land with Silas gone. Besides, she preferred baking over farming, and life had been easier for her and Gabby since they'd settled in. There had been a lot of changes, but changes that were better for both her and her five-year-old daughter. Changes that involved each of them becoming more independent. Despite her husband's absence, the Lord had provided abundantly for the two of them.

"Gabby, it's time to come down to the shop; you have to start your studies, and I have to open for the day. I'll need you to help me fill the display cases first."

Her daughter looked up from the doll she was sewing and nodded. "Yes, *Mamm.*"

"What are you making?"

Gabby showed it to her mother. "I'm making a doll—for a girl who might not have a doll."

Noel admired her daughter's stitching; she would make a fine living with her talent.

"It's nice; I'm sure whoever you give it to will be very happy."

Gabby smiled and put her project away and followed her mother down to the bakery.

CHAPTER THREE

HUNTER looked up toward the bakery when the lights came on inside; it was still a few minutes before nine o'clock, so he stayed in his car and watched for someone to open the door.

Within minutes, an Amish woman and a young girl about Raegan's age began to fill the display cases at the front counter with cookies, breads and pastries from racks they'd brought from the back area he assumed was the kitchen. He sat there watching as the young woman worked swiftly with the precision of a full crew of employees. She was making him tired just watching her. Of course, Holly had told him the same thing about himself many times, but when he was working on a piece of furniture, he would work until it was finished.

She looked out toward his truck and paused, her plain beauty immediately noticeable to Hunter. He imagined he towered over her by at least a foot, and her dainty features and narrow waist made him wonder if she ever ate any of her confections.

If I worked there, I'd be at least fifty pounds overweight—I wouldn't be able to help myself!

She had her hair pinned back in what Raegan called a *bun,* and she wore one of those white mesh bonnets the Amish women were famous for. He always wondered about them, but never cared to learn much about them beyond his sister telling him it was a prayer cap, but spelled with a "k".

She'd seen him sitting out front of her bakery; how long would he sit out here and wait?

She met his gaze; her eyes reminded him of sea glass, and her unblemished skin boasted a healthy, pink glow that swept across her cheeks as if painted there with the stroke of a fine-haired paintbrush. Would her porcelain skin be as soft as he imagined?

"I have many specials today," she said, pointing to the dry-erase boards behind her head. "Do you have something in mind, or do you need a minute to look over the displays?"

Her thick accent rolled off her tongue with a measure of charm that matched her smile.

He paused and their eyes fixed; he had no idea what intrigued him so much about her, but he couldn't pull his gaze away from hers.

She cast her eyes downward, breaking the spell between them. He pointed behind him at the window display, unable to find his voice.

"Did you want to enroll in the gingerbread class on Saturday morning? The gingerbread house you make is yours to take home with you. The cost of the class is ten dollars."

He shook his head. "I need three dozen gingerbread cookies for my daughter's class by Friday; I can't wait to learn how to bake them a day after I need them! Besides, the PTA president said anything the parents bring has to be homemade, and I can't bake. So, I thought I could buy those you have in the display."

She shook her head. "I can't sell you my display, and I'm afraid I don't have three dozen gingerbread cookies to sell you," she said.

"Didn't you say you're expected to bake them?"

He nodded slowly, pasting on his most charming smile.

"*Ach,* I won't help you deceive anyone; they will know I baked them, and I can't be part of such dishonesty."

He guffawed. "What? I thought this was a bakery! Don't you sell cookies to people who don't have time or don't know how—like me— to bake them? And aren't your cookies *homemade?*"

She nodded. "*Jah,* but it's dishonest for you to take my cookies to your *dochder's* class and tell them *you* baked them."

He shifted from one foot to the other. "Does this mean you won't sell me the cookies?"

"Even if I had enough to sell you, I couldn't do it in *gut* conscience."

He sighed. For someone as pretty as a fully-blossomed rose, she sure was full of thorns—and they were all sticking in his side at the moment.

He chuckled nervously. "You're kidding me, aren't you?"

She cast her eyes to the floor and shook her head. "I'll be more than happy to teach you, so you can make them yourself."

Hunter threw his hands up and swallowed the lump in his throat. "If her mother was still around to fix this, I wouldn't be in this mess; can't you make an exception just this once?"

She shook her head again.

Was she being smug, or was it just her way? He slid his business card across the counter and nodded politely. "Just in case you change your mind."

Without another word, he left the quaint little bakery that smelled of spices, and the company of the even spicier owner.

HUNTER sighed and tapped his hand on his steering wheel as he waited for his sister to answer the phone.

"Hey, little bro, how did it go?"

"She refused to help me!" he said, his voice raised.

"I suppose it is pretty last-minute, and she's probably got orders backed up," Holly said.

He shook his head as if she could see him. "No! She said she *refused* to help me!"

A moment of silence.

"Did she give you a reason?"

He fumed and pursed his lips just thinking about the woman making such statements about him when she knew nothing about his life.

"She said that would be cheating and deceptive of me to take cookies that *she* baked to the school when I was the one who was supposed to bake them."

"Oh."

"To make matters worse," he said, his jaw clenching. "She offered to teach me how to bake them myself."

Holly laughed. "Oh, I like her!"

"It's not funny, Holly, what am I going to do? I have to have these cookies baked in two days!"

She laughed again. "Then I suggest, little brother, that you swallow your pride and take the woman up on her offer!"

I'd rather take my chances with Kate's recipes," he said, clenching his jaw.

The last thing he wanted to do was to dig through Kate's recipes, which she'd hand-written each one. The house would smell of gingerbread and he feared he'd end up in a heap on the sofa eating junk food and feeling sorry for himself like a jilted teenager.

He'd walked out of the bakery without another word. Besides, he didn't have time to go to a cooking class; he had to have the cookies in two days. Even if she offered to teach him today, he didn't have time; he was already backed up with work orders for Christmas. Those people counted on him to make their rocking chairs and nativities, and other holiday items.

Then it hit him; how would he feel if someone had come to him with the same request as he'd just presented to the lovely Amish woman. He would no sooner want anyone to tell their loved ones they had made the signature piece of furniture he'd made.

I get it now, Lord. The whole "do unto others" thing.

He'd insulted her, and now he had to go back and apologize, or he'd never be able to live with himself.

CHAPTER FOUR

NOEL watched the handsome *Englisher* drive away and wished she hadn't spoken to him so firmly. Her back had automatically reared when he'd displayed the slightest hint he was willing to be dishonest. If there was one thing being married to Silas had taught her, it was to be suspicious of everyone—especially *Englishers*.

It was only cookies; so why had she reacted so harshly? Truth-be-told, she couldn't handle anymore deception in her life, and she'd developed a loathing she supposed for *English* men. Silas had instilled that in her, but she supposed all *Englishers* weren't the same, just as all Amish men were not the same. She'd made an unfair judgment of the man when he'd needed help, and if she ever saw him again—which wasn't likely, she'd have to remember to apologize.

Was it his attractive features that had made her feel so uncomfortable? For a fleeting moment, she'd imagined what it might be like to be in his strong arms, but she'd shamefully pushed away the thoughts just as swiftly as they'd entered her mind, fearful her lonely heart would betray her.

Perhaps the loss of her husband had affected her in ways she hadn't realized until that handsome *Englisher* entered her bakery and opened her eyes to it. She pushed down the worries and went about the task of filling her morning orders, wishing the stranger would return so she could apologize.

The jingling of the bells on the door brought her gaze up from her task of wiping the counter, and snow blew in through the door.

Becca, her young cousin and employee, stomped her boots on the mat in front of the door. "*Ach,* I think we're supposed to get several more inches of snow before the afternoon is over."

Noel forced a smile. "It won't make it easy for me to get rid of these orders; you know people tend to put the bakery last on their list, and if the weather is too bad, they don't show up for their orders. I wish they knew that cost me extra to make new cookies to replace their stale ones."

"Sell them; you know most will not show up, and you always hold back from people who are strong enough to brave the snowstorms."

Noel sighed. "I suppose you're right."

Becca waved a hand in front of her cousin's face. "That's not what's bothering you; don't tell me you're thinking about Silas. I know it's the holidays and you're lonely, but you need to put him out of your mind."

"I was sort of thinking about him, but not in the way you think," she said. "I wasn't mourning over him or missing him; I was comparing him—I guess."

Becca raised an eyebrow. "To who?"

"An *Englisher* who was in here earlier; he was trying to get me to bake three dozen gingerbread cookies for his *dochder's* class at her school."

Becca shrugged. "What's wrong with that? We could use the money; gingerbread is expensive—and this is a bakery, isn't it?"

"He wanted to pass them off as homemade."

Another shrug, followed by a shake of her head and widening eyes. "They *are* homemade; so, what's the problem?"

"He wanted the school to think *he* baked them; can you believe the nerve of some people?"

Becca nodded. "Now I get it; you can't get past the *little white lie.*"

Noel pursed her lips and scowled. "There's more to it than that."

Becca laughed as she put away her coat in the closet to the side of the front counter.

"He must have been handsome!"

"That isn't funny!" Noel said, stacking the festive, Christmas boxes they used for packaging the cookies.

"He must have been real handsome; you're blushing."

Noel put her back to her cousin, heat rising in her cheeks. "What he looks like has nothing to do with how I feel about this. You know I have trouble trusting—especially men—especially *English* men."

"Not every man is going to leave you the way Silas did," her cousin said. "How were you to know when you married him he wouldn't be with you for the rest of your life? I know that's how it should be, but sometimes it just doesn't work out that way."

"He didn't leave me the way he was supposed to—in death."

Becca gasped. "You would rather he died?"

"No! But honestly, it would have been easier to accept. At least that way, I'd know he had no choice. He chose to leave me for that wealthy, spoiled *English* woman, and he left me with the burden of all the shame. I can't even face the community—you know they all-but shunned me."

Becca put a hand on her shoulder. "They didn't shun you, but they haven't made it easy for you to be around them. They blame you, and I know that isn't fair. But you still have me."

Noel forced a smile. "Only until you get married; then you'll be too busy with a husband and wee ones to remember we are cousins."

"I don't know if that will happen anytime soon; look at me, I'm as plain as can be. No man will notice me—especially not in an Amish-run *English* bakery."

"Perhaps you should participate more in the youth events in the community," Noel said.

Becca cleared her throat and pointed across the street. "Speaking of events, I wonder what she'll ask you to volunteer for this time; do you want to hide? She's crossing the street."

Noel laughed. "No sense; she'll let herself in the back of the bakery like always, and she'll have me worn down before I can tell her no."

Brenda, the Chamber of Commerce president, wasn't a friendly woman, and she wasn't well-liked, but she did keep the small community profiting. Since Noel had joined, her business had increased, so she supposed an occasional favor couldn't hurt.

"I'm sure she wants a basket of free cookies for the Christmas auction, so she can have free things to raffle off to make money to cover the tree-lighting."

"We're about to find out!"

The door jingled and in walked Brenda with a stomp of her feet and an audible shiver.

"It's a cold one, today!" Brenda said, removing her hat and gloves. "How are you ladies this morning?"

"We are fine, *danki,*" Noel said. "You look cold; would you like a cup of cocoa?"

She nodded. "Yes, thank you."

Noel signaled to Becca, who went about the task behind the counter, while Noel offered Brenda a seat at one of the four small tables along the front window.

Brenda motioned for Noel to join her.

"I've come to ask a favor, but I don't want to offend you—or your beliefs."

Noel's heart thumped.

"My beliefs?"

"Your *religious* beliefs. I wouldn't ask, except I'm in an awful pickle."

She sounded so serious. Noel stared blankly, waiting for the woman to finish, and then take her foot out of her mouth.

"I need someone to play *Mary* in the Live Nativity in the park tonight."

Noel breathed a little easier. "Is that all?"

Brenda chortled. "Does that mean you'll do it?"

Noel nodded. "I'm a believer, if that was what you were worried about. I'll play the part."

Brenda put a hand to her chest. "Oh, of course you are; bless your heart."

Becca brought the woman her cocoa, and she held up a hand. "Can I get that to go? I have a few other businesses to hit up for *favors*."

She winked at Noel. "Oh, and one more thing; can I count on you for a couple dozen cookies for the silent auction? And a cake for the Cake-Walk booth would be nice, too."

"*Jah.* Anything else?*"

"Excellent, not a thing" she said, as Becca handed her the to-go cup. She rose from the chair and put her gloves and hat back on and headed for the door. She turned around just before exiting.

"I forgot to tell you the best part," she said with a mischievous smile. "That handsome-hunky widower, Hunter Darcy, is playing *Joseph!*"

CHAPTER FIVE

NOEL rummaged through the trash for the *Englisher's* business card. She'd been so irritated after he left earlier that morning that she tossed it in the trash.

"What are you looking for?" Becca asked.

Noel jumped up and sucked in her breath, putting a hand to her chest, her heart pounding. "I dropped something and now I can't find it."

Becca reached into her pocket and smiled as she held up the card. "Are you looking for this?"

Noel planted her fists on her hips and scowled. "You took that out of the trash?"

Becca wagged her finger at her. "The real question is, why did you put it in the trash?"

Noel fumed. "You give that back to me right now."

Becca laughed. "You are blushing! That's the second time today that this Mr. Darcy has caused you to blush. And according to Brenda, he's a handsome hunk!"

"And a widower," Noel said with downcast eyes. "I suppose that would explain a few things."

"Does it explain why you are blushing?"

Noel ignored her cousin and put on a pair of plastic gloves, and began boxing up the cookies for the silent auction.

HUNTER took notes as he watched the YouTube video once more. His sister was right about one thing; you could find an instructional video on YouTube on just about any subject. He chuckled inwardly as he watched the man mixing up the ingredients for gingerbread cookies.

If this guy can do it and make it look so easy, so can I.

He made himself a quick shopping list, closed his computer, and then shouldered out into the snow to the shopping center only a few blocks away. In the warmer months, he usually walked to the store, but today it was just a little bit too cold. He would have to remember to wear his long-johns tonight while he was volunteering for the live Nativity. Normally, he wouldn't volunteer for such things because it meant getting a sitter for Raegan. When Brenda from the Chamber had asked him, he was all too happy to volunteer. It was an honor to be asked, but more than that, she offered placement for his daughter as the shepherd boy. She had been so excited about it, and begged him to let her do it, explaining to him that it was good for her *acting* career.

He'd had to hold back laughter over his daughter's comments, but after watching her performance in the Nutcracker as one of the fairies, he'd have to say she was well on her way. Between that and her every-day dramatic performances at home over something as minute as getting ready for school in the morning, he'd have to say she was indeed a very good actress.

He parked his truck in a spot nearest the door and ran in to get the handful of ingredients. He'd almost made it to the checkout lane before he noticed Alice Parker walking in. He lowered his head, hoping if he didn't make eye-contact with her she'd leave him alone.

"Mr. Darcy," she called out to him.

No such luck.

"I'm so glad I caught you," she said, as she approached him.

He was in line and his things were already being rung up; there would be no escaping her until she was finished.

"I wanted to make sure you signed up for the auction," she said, winking at him.

"Yes, I am; I've entered a doll house I made."

Ms. Parker giggled. "I didn't mean the silent auction tonight; I meant the bachelor's auction on Friday night."

His heart slammed against his ribcage. "I didn't plan on participating in that one."

She pushed out her lower lip. "How else am I going to get a date with you, if I can't use my very generous alimony checks to buy one?"

His sister had told him she'd gotten a large sum of money from her husband when he'd divorced her, so he could run off and marry a much younger woman. He'd even agreed to file in Florida, where he'd run off to, just so she could collect the alimony. Had he done all that just to get away from her, or was he just that much of a jerk? Hunter suspected it might have been a mixture of both.

"I'm sorry, Ms. Parker, but I don't date; if I ever do date, it'll be in God's timing—not mine."

She curled up her lip at him for the second time today; it sent a wave of disgust through him. He smiled, nevertheless, but in a way, he hoped she wouldn't think he was interested in keeping her company.

"I wish I could convince you to change your mind," she said, followed by a nervous laughter.

"I'm actually working tonight as a volunteer at the live Nativity," he blurted out.

Now, he'd gone and let her know exactly where to find him; why did he have no defenses for this woman?

She looked at his purchases as the cashier put them in bags. "I see you're baking those cookies for the class party."

He wanted to snap at her and tell her he was doing what he said he was going to, but he held his tongue. He was not the type of man to speak harshly to anyone—especially a woman.

But even he had to admit, this one tested his patience.

The cashier finished bagging his things and he offered the very pushy Ms. Parker a kind smile and a nod before leaving the store.

Once he was outside, he pulled in a deep breath of the cold air, hoping it would cool his boiling blood. In some ways he felt sorry for her; it wasn't right what her husband had done to her, but he was not the one to put her back together; that was a job big enough that only God could fix it for her—and only if she let Him. The only thing he could do for her was to put her on his prayer list.

He shook off the uneasiness he felt and hopped into his truck with a determination to concentrate on his daughter's needs. She was who he lived for, and she was second only to God in his life. There just wasn't any room in his life for anyone else, and that was how he intended to keep it.

He drove home, resisting the urge to pester his sister again; he was a big boy who could solve his own problems. He had a new confidence, and he was going to bake those cookies, and they were going to be so good, he might just take them and show them off to that judgmental Amish woman.

Why should he care what she thought?

Because she was right. So why had that bothered him so much? She'd reprimanded him. Not in a demeaning sort of way—more of a conviction—a challenge to do the right thing. Kate used to do that. Sometimes it would make him a little angry, but once he thought it through, he always realized she was right. It was almost as if she could look right through his soul and see where he needed a little molding. The Amish woman had done that to him. It wasn't so much the words she'd chosen, but more her mannerisms. It had snuck up on him so quickly, he hadn't realized until he'd left the bakery.

Lord, help me to let go of my pride and go to that woman and apologize.

CHAPTER SIX

HUNTER unpacked his groceries and organized the ingredients according to the recipe. Who knew such a simple cookie needed so many spices?

Luckily, he had a large bowl he used for popcorn. He needed a cup; his extra coffee mug would do. Then there were the spoons; what was the difference between a teaspoon and a tablespoon? He opened his silverware drawer; there were small spoons they used for cereal, and a few his wife said were for soup. Those had to be the right ones, didn't they? They weren't fancy round ones like it showed on the video, but they looked about the same size. No need to buy more stuff just to bake some cookies.

Since his move, he'd gotten rid of most of the dishes, since there was limited cupboard space in the loft above the workshop. Kate had so many things for baking and cooking, and he just didn't see the necessity for all those dishes. He'd had the sense to keep the round pan used for cooking frozen pizzas; it would make a great cookie sheet.

He checked the recipe once more, noting that the butter or shortening needed to be melted. Deciding to skip that step, believing it wasn't that important, and it would take him even longer, he measured it out by the markings on the side of the paper wrapper that covered the stick of butter. Then he poured the molasses into the coffee cup to measure it. Next, he packed the brown sugar into the coffee cup and then spooned it into the bowl, then cracked an egg and dropped it in the bowl. Last, he filled the coffee cup halfway with water and poured it into the bowl with the rest of the ingredients. He mashed and stirred and mashed and stirred until it was mixed.

Glancing once more at the recipe, he remembered in the video that he was supposed to sift the dry ingredients. One quick glance around his kitchen told him he had no such utensil.

"Time to improvise," he said, as he picked up a splatter screen he put over his frying pan to cook bacon.

It was flat, but it would work.

He placed the screen over the bowl, and one by one, he dumped 6 cups of flour onto the screen, shaking it back and forth. By this time, there was probably more flour on the counter than there was in the bowl. This did not discourage him.

"That looks to be about a half cup worth, he said with a chuckle. "I'll just add another half cup to make up for the mess."

After sifting that last bit of flour, he took the large spoon and began to stir the flour. Afterward, he used the big and small spoons to measure out the spices and the baking powder, and then stirred those in. Once it was smooth, he looked again at the directions to make sure he hadn't missed anything.

"Who says men can't follow directions?" he said with a chuckle.

Glancing at the clock, he knew he did not have time to wait three hours for the dough to chill in the refrigerator. If he did, he'd be late to car line to pick up Raegan. From there, his day would only go downhill. He'd be late to the live

Nativity, and he would never get his project to the park for the festival of lights in time for the silent auction. That dollhouse was his calling card. It was a way for him to spread the word about his business, and he prayed it would help him sell the two dozen dollhouses he'd made in anticipation of the Christmas sale. He'd gone out on a limb making those dollhouses, hoping his hunch would pay off.

He glanced at the clock once more; no matter how many times he added it up, there just wasn't enough time to wait for the dough to cool. He'd have to roll it out, cut the cookies, and get them baking. Once again, he looked around for something he could use as a rolling pin. Then it dawned on him; he had tons of "rolling pins" in his workshop. After all, a dowel rod was the same as a rolling pin, wasn't it? Nevertheless, it would work.

Hunter ran down the stairs and into his workshop, grabbed the shortest dowel rod, and then ran back upstairs.

He paused. "Maybe I should wash it first."

He ran the stick of wood under the faucet and even used a little drop of soap. Once he was satisfied that it was clean, he dried it off with the kitchen towel and doused it with flour the same way he'd seen the baker do it in the video. Then he mashed the dough with his hands, covering the sticky dough with flour and rolled it out with the dowel rod. Luckily, it only stuck to his makeshift rolling pin a little bit. Next, he went about the task of cutting out the shapes. He hadn't thought that it was necessary to spend extra money on pre-shaped cutters, so he set about the task with a kitchen knife. After all, he was a carpenter, and he cut out shapes all day long with his tools. Cookie dough was a lot softer than wood. He stuck the knife in the dough, and it didn't take him long to realize that the dough was bending. Maybe this wasn't easier. What was he going to do?

Then he remembered the Play-Doh gift Raegan had gotten for the *Secret Santa* gift exchange at school. It was a gingerbread kit his daughter had picked out, and he had a hunch it was because she wanted one for herself. He knew it had a gingerbread man cookie cutter inside the box. He hurried into her room and picked up the box that was on her dresser.

It had plastic around it. Would she notice if he opened it? It wasn't too late to buy another kit; the gift exchange was Friday, the day of the party. That way, he could put this one aside and put it under the tree for Raegan.

A tree.

They hadn't gotten one last year; he was too busy mourning for Kate, and had not been able to do any more than was necessary for Raegan. His sister had filled in the gap with her

large tree and presents, and baking cookies—
things he should have done, but just couldn't.

This year, he was going to make up for
it—starting with the cookies for her class party
on Friday.

He blew out a heavy sigh as he looked at
the box in his hands. "So much for saving
money, but this is an emergency!"

He took out his pocket knife and slid it
along the inside edge between the top and
bottom of the box, and then removed the
plastic.

"She's a kid; she won't notice if the
plastic is off the box! I'll use the cookie cutter
and put it back before she gets home."

He smiled proudly as he lifted the top off
and reached for the gingerbread cookie cutter.
It was kind of small, but it would have to do.
He was, after all, being inventive—and frugal
at the same time.

He took the cookie cutter back to the kitchen and began the task of cutting the cookies. With the oven preheating per the instructions, it was only a matter of time before he had cookies for Raegan's entire class.

If that Amish woman could see me now!

He chuckled to himself. Why did he care so much what she thought of him? He would deny any attraction to her if anyone asked. He would say it was because she'd called him out for trying to get away with something, and now he wanted to prove to her that he could handle his business. If truth-be-told, her opinion of him mattered. It was foolish, but he just couldn't shake the feeling.

The first gingerbread man wouldn't come away from the cutter. He pounded it on the counter trying to shake it loose, so he pushed it through with his fingers and the head fell off. He grumbled inwardly and pinched the head back on the body. It wasn't perfect, but it was a start.

He dusted the top of the sticky dough with more flour and then tried again. This time the cookie came loose and so did the next and the rest that followed.

He smiled as he placed them on the pizza pan and then he put them in the oven. He looked at the clock, noting it would take him at least twenty minutes to box up the dollhouse so he could take it to the silent auction tonight.

The recipe called for ten to twelve minutes at 350 degrees, so he turned the temperature down to 300 degrees thinking that should buy him an extra five minutes or so. He left the kitchen and rushed down the stairs to his workshop. In the small showroom, his father waited on a customer. He had been fortunate for his dad's support, and they'd made room for him on the other side of the large loft apartment up above the shop. Not only was he a built-in babysitter when he was needed for short periods of time, he was the perfect employee, and the only family his daughter had left in the area. With his sister now in another state, the men were on their own. His dad claims he likes it that way because she fusses over him too much, but Hunter knew the old man missed her just as much as he did—especially for this sort of problem.

He knew there would come a day when he would have to fend for himself, and so far, he wasn't doing too badly. Now that he had the gingerbread cookie problem under control, he was well on his way to total independence.

"Son," his dad called to him from the showroom. "This gentleman has some questions I can't answer."

Hunter walked over to them and shook the customer's hand.

"I know it's last-minute, but I'd like to know if you could make me a toboggan or sled long enough for three kids; all I can find these days are short sleds and those single sleds. I have a set of four-year-old triplets—all boys, and would like to be able to pull them on it in the snow."

Hunter smiled. "Sounds like you've got your hands full!"

The man smiled and nodded.

"I could have it for you by next Friday, the twenty-second; that's three days before Christmas, so you'll have plenty of time to relax."

"That is more than I expected; thank you!"

Hunter grabbed a piece of paper from the counter and drew a quick sketch. "I could enclose the back with a rail—like this, if you want," he said, showing the man. "I could put a rudder on the front, and put runners on the bottom more like a sled. I can attach a long, heavy rope here, so you can pull it, and if they should venture down any hills in the future, they can pull the rope up and use it to steer it."

"I like the idea of a custom-made toboggan—sled, but how much more would that cost me?"

"I'm not going to sugar-coat it; it would be a hundred dollars; does that fit in your budget?" Hunter asked.

The customer shook his head vigorously and smiled, offering his hand to Hunter. "That's a lot less than I expected, so I'm happy."

He pulled out an order form from the tray at the counter and began to fill out the details of the order, such as materials and labor cost.

Then he slid it over to the customer. "If you'll fill out the top part and include your phone number, I'll be able to call you when it's ready to be picked up."

He filled in all the spaces and handed it back to Hunter, and the two shook hands. "Thank you," he said. "You've just made sure my three boys have a fun Christmas—the sort of Christmas I had when I was a kid."

"You be safe out there; that snow is really coming down," he said as his customer left the shop.

Hunter snapped his fingers. "He's given me a great idea!"

His dad peered over his glasses at him.

"Remember how much I used to love sledding and skating when I was a kid?"

His dad nodded. "You wore me out!"

"I've been wondering what I could do to keep Raegan busy over Christmas break, and she's been bugging me about all the activities going on downtown, such as the candle-lit skating party on Saturday at Goose Pond, and sledding down the big hill on the other side of the pond. I think I'm going to show her an old-fashioned Christmas. We can make snowmen and snow-angels, and even have a snowball fight."

His dad smiled and patted him on the back. "You're wearing me out just thinking about it."

It would be their second Christmas without Kate, and he'd been such a mess the first year, he was grateful Raegan was still young enough he'd been able to fool her by going through the motions of Christmas, though his heart had not been in it.

This year was going to be different; they were going to get a tree, and they were going to have fun.

His dad lifted his head and sniffed the air. "Son, are you burning something?"

CHAPTER SEVEN

"Oh no! My cookies!"

HUNTER ran up the stairs to the loft, the smoke alarm going crazy and the kitchen was filled with smoke. He coughed as he made his way to the stove and turned it off.

Then he went over to the sliding glass door to the balcony and threw it open to air out the room. Once he could see well enough, he realized there was nothing on fire, but when he opened the door to the oven, his first batch of cookies was nothing but gingerbread man-shaped charcoal.

He dropped the pizza pan on the top of the stove and went over to the window with the kitchen towel to finish airing out the apartment. The smoke alarm finally stopped beeping, and by this time, his father was hollering up the stairs.

He went to the doorway. "Everything's fine, Pop," he said. "I burned the cookies, but I'll bake another batch."

"I told you to listen to your sister and take that Amish woman's class," his dad hollered up the stairs.

"I can't, Pop; her class is on Saturday and I need the cookies Friday morning!" he hollered back.

He tossed the still smoking cookies into the trash and put the receptacle on the balcony.

Then he turned the oven back on and set about the task of rolling out a new batch.

This time, he would set the stove on the right temperature—and not think he has extra time! He would set the timer on his phone and when it went off, he'd have perfect cookies. He slathered more flour on the sticky dough. He supposed he probably should have put the leftover dough back in the fridge in between baking, but he'd not make the same mistake twice; it would get put away this time.

Once the new batch of cookies was in the oven and his timer set, he ran back down to the shop to box up the dollhouse for the silent auction. He had just enough time to bake this last batch of cookies before he had to pick up Raegan at school.

His list of things to do for the day had somehow increased to an out-of-control number. How did mothers manage this stuff and make it look so easy? Raising a child on your own was hard work! His thoughts automatically turned to the Amish woman in the bakery. What was her story? Was she a widow too? She had to be; from what little he knew of their culture, they didn't believe in divorce, and they lived by a strict rule of purity that had long-since left the *English* world from years-gone-by. The young girl he'd seen at the bakery seemed to be the same age as Raegan, yet she worked alongside her mother and appeared to be very well behaved. Raegan was a good kid, but he was certain she could never display that sort of discipline—not even if he threatened to ground her.

He chuckled inwardly wondering how Raegan would react if he should ask the Amish Woman out to coffee. Would she understand?

He had to stop thinking so much; he was getting way ahead of himself. With the dollhouse boxed up, he let his dad know he was going back upstairs to check on his cookies.

His alarm went off; he'd made it this time! He rushed up the stairs and went straight to the kitchen and opened the oven.

They looked perfect!

He chuckled; he was proud of himself. He'd done it—and without help from the Amish woman!

He rolled out several paper towels onto the counter and then used the spatula to remove them from the pan. They could stay out and cool while he picked Raegan up from school. But before that, he had to clean off the gingerbread cookie cutter he'd taken from her *Secret Santa* gift and return it to the box, so she wouldn't know he used it.

Then he stopped what he was doing; that Amish woman was right about him! His heart sunk to his feet. He was everything she said about him; he was deceptive and didn't mind fooling people with his antics, as long as it all turned out okay. But was it okay?

He wasn't a bad guy; he had a lot of good qualities, but he didn't mind getting away with something if it benefitted him.

Was he a bad example to Raegan?

A lump formed in his throat as he slipped the cookie cutter back into the Play-Doh Holiday Gingerbread Kit.

Tomorrow, he would make up for it; today, all he could do was to get through the rest of it the best he could. The remainder of his day was overscheduled, but tomorrow, when there was time, he'd fix this. He'd fix everything.

"RAEGAN, put your things away before you get a snack," Hunter said as they walked in the door.

Her eyes gleamed as she looked toward the kitchen, her breath catching.

"You made cookies!" she squealed.

"I made those for your class!"

She turned around and pushed out her lower lip. "Can I have one, please, Daddy?"

He nodded, and she threw off her coat and dropped to the floor to remove her boots. Dumping them in a heap with her coat, she ran to the counter and grabbed one.

"Don't you want to ice them first?" he asked, stopping her before it reached her mouth.

She shrugged and bit into it, pulling it away with a squeal.

Hunter rushed to her side. "What's wrong?"

She spit out her front tooth, and Hunter thought he was going to faint. He grabbed a paper towel and took it from her and cleaned it off. "What happened? Let me see."

He put his hand at her chin and lifted.

79

"It was the loose one, Daddy; now the tooth fairy can give me some money!"

She flashed him a toothless grin.

He supposed it was due to happen. His sister had warned him that one day they lose their first tooth and then the next, it seems you're shopping for wedding dresses.

"Oh, my little girl is growing up so fast."

She giggled. "I'm only five, Daddy. I think it might take me a while before I'm as tall as you."

He scooped her up in his arms. "And you're so wise, too!"

She hugged him and giggled as she wriggled out of his arms. He set her feet on the floor and looked at her tooth. Then he wadded another paper towel and handed it to her. "Bite down on this, it'll stop the bleeding."

She squealed. "Oh no! It's bleeding?"

"It's okay, Raegan. It doesn't hurt, does it?"

She settled down and thought about it. "It did when I tried to take a bite out of these hard cookies!"

He grabbed the cookie from her and tried to break it, and then pounded it on the counter.

Nothing.

"Great! I made gingerbread bricks!"

Reagan reached up her arms and he bent to hug her. "I'm sorry, Pumpkin."

She giggled. "I'm not! Now I get to put my tooth under my pillow for the Tooth Fairy! Remember, you told me, Daddy, she gives out five whole dollars for your first tooth!"

He nodded. "I did say that, didn't I?"

He took it over to the small desk in the corner of the living room and grabbed an envelope and a pen. "Let's put it in an envelope and write the date on it so the Tooth Fairy knows it's a new tooth. We'll even put on the outside that it's the first one—just in case she's not sure."

He had to laugh inwardly. It was a small deception—just like the whole *Santa* thing, but it was something that made her happy. Were there some instances where a *little white lie* was okay? No, the cookie thing was not the same. Granted, those cookies meant a lot to her, but they meant even more to him. If he couldn't solve a small crisis like this, he was in for it when the big stuff his sister warned him about would come along.

He had to figure this out, but he couldn't do it alone. He'd have to lean on his sister a little more, but from a distance.

"Raegan, go rinse your mouth out with water in the bathroom, and then get started on your homework; I'll help you in a minute."

Once she disappeared he pulled his phone from his pocket and pressed the avatar with Holly's picture on it.

After two rings, she answered. "What happened now?"

Hunter sighed. "Why do you do that?"

"What?"

"Assume something is wrong, even if you're right!" he said.

Holly laughed. "Because it's after three o'clock and you've probably not been home with Raegan more than ten minutes."

Another heavy sigh. "My cookies turned out to be hard as bricks and Raegan lost her tooth trying to bite into one!"

She gasped. "I hope it was her loose tooth in the front!"

He waved his hand in the air as if she could see him. "Yes, it was, but that's not the point; my gingerbread cookies broke her tooth.

I burned the first batch, and this second one I was so proud of, turned out to be hard as bricks. I don't understand what I did wrong."

"Gingerbread is temperamental to work with. That's why I've never attempted it. You took on a big project, little brother, and you either have to see it through or give up. You're sweating over this way too much."

He put his hand to his chin and smoothed over his goatee with his thumb.

"What do you suggest?"

"I don't know why you're stressing over this, Hunter; just go to the store and buy a roll of that ready-made cookie dough and slice it up and bake it. You'll have cookies for the party that your child won't break anymore of her teeth on, and no one will ever know any different unless *you* tell them."

Hunter ran a hand through his thick, brown hair. "I'll know, and that is deceptive, and I can't do it; what kind of example is that for Raegan?"

"Coming from someone who was totally willing to un-box store-bought cookies and pass them off as his own just yesterday, I don't understand why you won't do just that."

He cleared his throat and pushed at the kitchen rug with the toe of his boot.

"That was before I met that Amish woman."

Holly chuckled. "Oh, I see; she really got to you, didn't she? She must be really pretty!"

He pounded his fist on the counter. "Her looks have nothing to do with this."

"Wow, that pretty, huh?" Holly asked, letting out a giggle.

"She got me to see that if I show Raegan that it's okay to lie and take credit for something you didn't take any pride in making, then I've shown her it's okay to cheat your way through life. I never realized such a little thing mattered so much."

Silence.

"Say something," Hunter said.

"I don't know what else to say, except I think you're finally growing up! I'm proud of you for wanting to teach your daughter right from wrong. Being a parent is a big responsibility, and it's just as hard making those tough decisions as it is making the small ones. I think this world could do with a little more of that kind of honesty."

"Thanks, but honesty won't get me out of this jam."

"Buy the Amish cookies and tell the truth when you take them to the school if it means that much to you."

"I'm not sure she'll even sell me any, and I'm not sure I can bring myself to asking," he grumbled.

"You better make up your mind fast," Holly said.

He hung up the phone after thanking her. What for, he wasn't sure, other than being a better sounding board than the four walls.

His only worry now was if he had enough guts to go crawling back to the Amish woman for help.

CHAPTER EIGHT

"RAEGAN, let's go!" her grandfather said. "Your dad is putting the dollhouse in the truck, so we better get down there."

"Just a minute, Poppy," she said with a gurgle. "I'm trying to brush my teeth and it's not easy now with my tooth gone."

She finished rinsing and then ran out to the living room to show her grandpa.

"How do they look?" she asked with a bright smile.

"They look clean!" he said, pulling her face into his hands and kissing her on the forehead. "Let's go before your daddy hollers up the stairs after us."

She giggled and pushed her feet into her boots, and then pulled on her coat. He handed her mittens, hat and scarf to her that were hanging on the hooks near the door, and they were on their way.

"I brushed my teeth, Daddy, wanna see?" Raegan asked as she bounded into the garage. She smiled brightly for him.

"They're beautiful—just like you!" He scooped her up in his arms and put her in the back seat of the truck and buckled her into her booster seat.

"Let's get going, Squirt, I don't want to be late."

NOEL walked through the park, holding hands with Gabby. Overhead, little round light bulbs strung along the walkways lit up the entire park as if it was daytime. Candy cane arches created a canopy over the path, and all the pine trees sparkled with twinkling, colored lights. Though the path had been shoveled, light snow dusted the sidewalk, the townspeople leaving warm footprints on the cement. It had warmed up a little and the snow was wet coming down. She supposed the rise in temperature had brought so many out tonight, but the events helped raise funds for the week-long festivities.

In the center of the park, in the gazebo, a brass band played Christmas Carols, and Noel couldn't help but feel more at home amongst the *Englishers*; they were less judgmental than her own people had been after Silas had left her. She knew that divorce was more prominent among the *English*, but that didn't mean she agreed with it. On the other hand, she was grateful for the divorce when she discovered he'd been unfaithful.

She shook off the feelings of sadness; tonight, was going to be a festive night and she was determined to have fun. It had been two years and she'd not seen him since; she preferred it that way, and it was time for her to move on with her life and start thinking of her future. Her gaze followed the path toward the Nativity. Constructed from old barn wood from the looks of it, a bright star lit up over the center of the front of the barn-like structure. Inside, a wooden feedbox full of straw held a doll wrapped in white linen. Men dressed in shepherd's clothing held staffs in their hands and men dressed as the three Wise Men held trinkets in their hands that represented the spices they'd brought for the infant Savior.

"YOU!" Hunter said as he saw Noel at the live Nativity. "You're playing Mary?"

She nodded, the look on her face told him he'd probably offended her and that another apology was in order.

"I didn't mean that the way it sounded. I was just surprised, that's all," Hunter said. "I thought we had different *faith.*"

Another stricken look.

"I'm sorry; I'll just be quiet now—long enough to take my foot out of my mouth."

She smiled.

"*Jah,* we do share the same faith, and I am playing Mary,*"* she said, then pointed to her daughter and cousin. "This is my *dochder*— daughter, Gabby, and my cousin, Becca."

Hunter cleared his throat and made a jerky arm movement toward his family. "Oh—this is my daughter, Raegan," he said, pulling her toward him. "She's playing the Shepherd boy."

The two girls waved and smiled.

"It's nice to meet you, Miss Raegan," Noel said. "It looks like you're missing the same tooth as my Gabby."

"It was loose for two whole weeks, but my Daddy's gingerbread cookies made my tooth come out!" Raegan said before Hunter could stop her.

Noel smiled and bit her bottom lip.

"They were as hard as bricks!" Raegan finished.

"Cookie bricks?" Noel asked, suppressing a smile.

"Gingerbread cookie-bricks," Hunter said with a chuckle.

Then he turned to his dad and introduced him.

His father smiled and took Noel's hand briefly. "You didn't tell me you knew such a beautiful woman," he said.

Hunter could feel the heat rising in his cheeks, and he was grateful for the cold breeze that had likely already turned them pink.

"Pop, you might want to hang out at the Bingo tables inside the pavilion and get out of this wind. I'll come get you in an hour when my shift is up at this booth."

The old man winked. "I might be a rich man by the time Bingo is over and start planning a trip to Florida where it's warm!" he said with a shiver.

"Let's get into costume, shall we? It looks like the others are all ready to begin."

Brenda had told them there was a box inside the manger where they would find their costumes. He very quickly located the bag marked *shepherd boy,* and handed it to Reagan, who was too busy petting the live sheep. The burro hee-hawed, and she jumped and squealed.

Noel put a hand on his nose and showed Raegan. "He won't hurt you, honey," she said gently.

Hunter stood back and watched his daughter take to the Amish woman, whose name he still didn't know, for some reason. How had it not come up?

As he watched her work with Raegan, he couldn't help but be drawn to her even more than when he'd first met her this morning. He lifted his eyes heavenward.

Twice in one day, Lord; are you trying to tell me something?

Raegan giggled as the donkey nibbled at her hat. Noel handed her a handful of straw and showed her how to feed him. More giggles erupted from his daughter. Would Kate approve of such a woman to take her place as wife to him and mother to her daughter? He took a deep breath and let it out with a whoosh. He was getting way ahead of himself thinking such thoughts. Watching her with Raegan, he just couldn't help himself. She had a plain beauty that could only compare to one woman—his Kate.

Hunter snapped his attention away from the Amish woman long enough to put on his costume. The Wise men approached them and introduced themselves.

"I'm Noel Fisher," the Amish woman told them.

So that was her name; what a beautiful name. He supposed that explained the name of her bakery. He had to assume the way she spelled bakery was in the Dutch-German dialect—he wasn't exactly sure what language she spoke, but that was what he'd heard.

Thankfully, her English was well-understood, though he had to admit, he liked her accent.

"Shall we take our places?" one of the Wise Men suggested.

Noel finished putting on the robe and headdress and picked up the babe lying in the makeshift manger, and Hunter couldn't help but think how angelic she looked. He took his place next to her, unsure of what he was supposed to do, until Raegan came up from behind them and poked her head up between them.

She looked up at him and whispered. "You're supposed to put your arm around Mary, Daddy—to show you love her."

She grabbed his arm and tried to put it around Noel's shoulder. He tried to resist her, but she was very insistent. "Rae, you're supposed to be herding the sheep," he said, hoping to distract her.

"And you're supposed to show how much you love Mary and Baby Jesus; you have to do your job, Daddy."

He flashed Noel an apologetic look, while the Wise Men snickered to the side of them. "You're not helping," he whispered to them.

"If it was me," one of them said. "I'd have to agree with your daughter—provided the lady didn't mind."

Noel kept her gaze to the ground; he wished he could do the same.

"Raegan, maybe you want to go inside and hang out with Poppy instead of being out here in the cold," he offered her.

She nodded. "Yes, because this is boring!"

Noel's daughter came running up to the Nativity structure. "We got you some hot cocoa, *Mamm,* so you won't be cold out here."

She looked at Hunter. "My cousin, Becca, works at the bakery with me, but she also babysits for me; would you like her to take your daughter with mine to get some hot cocoa?"

Raegan pulled on his sleeve and swung from side to side. "Can I please go with them, Daddy?"

He nodded. "Are you sure it won't be too much for you?"

Becca shook her head. "I'm used to watching many nieces and nephews at once; she won't be a problem."

He took the costume, which she was quickly shedding. "You stay with them, and mind Miss Becca."

"Don't worry, Daddy," she said.

Gabby took one hand and Becca took the other, and they were gone before he could say another word to her.

Lord, please watch over her.

"I'm so sorry about her trying to get me to put my arm around you."

She smiled, keeping her gaze lowered. "Out of the mouths of babes!"

He chuckled. "You're not kidding; I thought for sure she was going to have us married for real before the night was over."

More snickering from the Wise Men.

He cleared his throat and took his place next to Noel, determined to keep quiet so he didn't end up with both feet in his mouth.

CHAPTER NINE

RAEGAN ran up to her dad at the Nativity just as he was putting away his costume; it had been a long and silent night for him, and not in a good way. He'd tried hard to keep his mind on task, but standing so close to the lovely Noel made his head spin. He was sure God was either laughing at him or ashamed of him for being so distracted.

How could he help himself? She smelled of cinnamon and cloves—like gingerbread— but certainly not his gingerbread bricks!

The cookies! He'd forgotten to ask her if she'd bake them, but now Rae was back and so was her daughter, Gabby, and her cousin, Becca. He couldn't ask in front of everyone— especially if her answer would be no again. Perhaps he would just wait until tomorrow morning after he dropped Rae off at school. Then, he would go back in the bakery—maybe take her a peace offering. But what?

A dollhouse? Yes! He would take a dollhouse for Gabby. Surely, she couldn't say no to a gift for her daughter. It was finally settled in his mind, and now he could relax and enjoy the rest of his evening with Raegan.

"What do you say about getting Poppy from the bingo tables and we can take a carriage ride around the park?" he asked his daughter.

"Can Gabby come with us, Daddy?" she begged, pushing out her lower lip. "She's my best friend."

Best friends? They've only been gone for a little over an hour!

"We're practically sisters," Raegan said.

His heart hit his ribs with a thud. That child was going to give him a heart attack, and he was too young for that. He'd been thinking practically the same thoughts—and he was too *old* for that. Maybe he should have kept his own thoughts from wondering about what it would be like to have Noel as a mother for Rae.

Noel surprised him by putting a hand on his arm. "Breathe, Mr. Darcy, that sort of talk is normal for little girls; if you don't breathe, you're going to faint. You're as white as the snow."

"That's really normal for her to get so *attached* so quickly?" he whispered back.

Like he had *any* room to talk!

"*Jah,* don't let it worry you, or you'll worry yourself sick."

He put a hand over his chest and breathed in deeply. "I think I already am; how am I ever going to get through all the rest of her stages? The only time I feel like I'm doing okay is when she's sleeping peacefully in her bed at night—no crisis, nothing broken, she doesn't have a care in the world—and she's quiet!"

Noel laughed, and it made his heart skip a beat. She really was beautiful.

Reagan was suddenly back at his side, yanking on his arm. "Can my sister go with me?"

How could he say no to her?

"I can't answer for Gabby; I'm not her daddy,"

"Sure, you are! She's my sister, remember?"

I walked—no, jumped, right into that one, didn't I?

"I hate to say no to the girls," Noel said. "But I fear your heart can't take anymore of her innocent, childish comments. She doesn't mean anything by them; she's just excited, that's all."

The girls joined hands and skipped ahead of them a little, Becca fast on their heels as they walked up under candy cane arches toward the gazebo. The band still played, and he wished they were playing something he could dance to—such as a waltz, but he doubted Noel was much of a dancer.

"I guess maybe I should sit in on her class once in a while—sort of see what else I'm missing when she's around other children. There's one girl in her class who bosses her around, and I suspect there could be a little bullying involved, but knowing her mother—

well, I doubt she would be much help—she's more like part of the problem. The worst part is, Raegan desperately wants to be this little girl's friend. But I've just never heard Ragan talk like this before—not calling another child her sibling when she has none, but she has cousins."

He had no idea why he was confiding in the woman, but it was nice to get a woman's point of view. There was only so many problems his sister could diagnose for him from such a long distance.

"You shouldn't worry about Raegan; I can see she's a strong girl, and her only fault seems to be she's very trusting and very friendly," Noel said.

"The friendly part she gets from me, but don't ask where she gets the trust from because I have problems trusting, and I don't want her to get hurt."

That was too much to say, but he couldn't take it back now. She was making it too easy for him to confide in her, and he was acting lonely and desperate. Perhaps he should excuse himself from her company before he made a complete fool of himself.

"Mr. Darcy!" a female voice said from behind them.

He cringed; he knew that voice.

Alice Parker.

Jenna ran up to the girls and pulled their hands apart. "Hey," she said to Gabby. "She's *my* friend."

Hunter took a step forward and Noel put her hand in front of his chest to stop him. "Give her a chance to handle it," she whispered.

Raegan put her hands on her hips. "I'm not going to be your friend anymore if you're not nice to my sister."

"Sister, huh?" Alice asked, sarcasm and fake laughter dripping from her tone. "Don't tell me you ran off and got married today without telling me! I hope you wouldn't break my heart like that."

Hunter turned to face her, but averted his gaze. What he saw in that split second was too much for any man who wasn't her husband to see. Her parka was longer than her skirt, her black leather boots up to her knees, and her chest poured out of the top of her shirt. Her perfume was enough to choke a man, and her lipstick so bright it could blind him.

He turned to Noel and flashed her a *forgive me* look.

"Ms. Parker, I'd like you to meet Noel; she runs the bakery downtown. And yes, we did get married just this afternoon!"

Noel tucked her arm in the crook of his elbow and smiled.

Alice huffed and narrowed her eyes, then curled her lip at Noel. "I can't believe you'd marry an *Amish* woman!"

"What man wouldn't want to marry such a *virtuous* woman?" Hunter asked.

"You really like that *Plain Jane* look?" she shrieked.

Hunter put his arm around Noel and pulled her close. "I do—I suppose that's why I said *I do!*"

Alice stomped her foot and growled. "I've never been so humiliated in all my life!" she stormed off, yanking Jenna by the arm and dragging her along with her when she left.

Hunter cleared his throat and patted Noel's hand. "Sorry about the deception," he said.

"I suppose there's room for exceptions to that rule," she said, smiling. "Besides, you looked like you needed to be rescued."

He chuckled. "Boy did I ever! She's been *after* me most of the school year; she seems to have it in her head that I'm a character from a book. I've suffered the teasing all my life, but there comes a time in a man's life when it's time for women to stop making him part of a fairytale."

She raised an eyebrow and smiled. "You mean you're not the *real* Mr. Darcy?"

"You know the story?"

She bit her lip. "I do know how to read, Mr. Darcy."

He put a hand over his heart and stopped walking, so he could look at her. "I didn't mean it like that; I just wasn't sure if you were *allowed* to read romance novels. I mean, I know Pride and Prejudice is a classic, but I thought you were only allowed to read your Bible."

"There is some truth to that, but I've always been a bit of a rebel. I'm sure every girl dreams of having her very own *Mr. Darcy.*"

She blinked away snowflakes that fell on her lashes, and he wanted to wipe them for her—just so he could touch her soft cheek.

"I guess I owe you one."

"I didn't do anything except keep quiet and go along with you," she said. "I'm just glad the girls were far enough ahead of us that they didn't hear that; I wouldn't want them to become confused."

"I'll admit, I'm feeling a little confused," he said. "Maybe not confused, but conflicted."

She lowered her gaze. "I'll admit, I have to agree with you on that."

He put his hand over his heart again and smiled. "Can we start over? I'd like us to be friends."

He didn't dare offer her more for fear he'd run her off. Truth was, he wanted to take her out for coffee—just the two of them so he could get to know her better. There was just something about her he couldn't get out of his mind.

She smiled. "*Jah,* I'd like that."

Raegan and Gabby ran up to them. "Hurry, Daddy, here comes the carriage, and I want to ride in it."

She pulled on his arm. "Did you know Gabby has her own horse and buggy, and she told me I could ride in it anytime I want to."

He looked at Noel. "Is that true?"

She nodded and laughed. "I do have one; it's not fancy like that white carriage, and my horse doesn't have a pretty red plume on his head, but I do have sleigh bells around his neck."

He chuckled. "Can I tell you a little secret? I've always wanted to drive one of those!"

"We can take mine once around the park if you'd like," she said. "I think the rented carriage is twenty-dollars."

"Ouch!" he said. "You should rent yours out too!"

"I've thought about it, but I would feel unsafe going alone; I'm the only parent Gabby has now."

He understood that worry.

"Maybe we could go into business together," he said with a chuckle. "I'll do the driving, and we split the profits three ways."

She flashed him a half-frown, half-smile. "Three ways?"

"Your horse has to be fed, doesn't he?"

She laughed. "*Jah,* he does."

"I'm friends with Mayor Abbott; I could probably get us a permit tomorrow," Hunter said. "We could bring in some nice profits between now and Christmas."

She giggled. "Shouldn't you learn how to drive it first?"

He puffed up his chest. "How hard could it be?"

CHAPTER TEN

HUNTER took the reins and tapped them on the horse's flank just a little harder than Noel had instructed him.

The buggy jolted forward; Noel grabbed his arm and squealed.

Laughter erupted from the back of the buggy. "That was fun, Daddy!"

No, it wasn't! How do I control this animal without looking like a total fool?

Hunter pulled back on the reins, trying to control the horse, but he seemed to have a mind of his own.

"Ease up on the reins a little," Noel said, still squeezing his arm. "Give him a little slack."

He did as she told him to; he was in no position to argue with her about it.

The horse slowed his pace and Hunter let out the breath he'd been holding in.

"Are you sure I don't need a special license to drive this?" he asked.

Noel shook her head. "I have a license for the back of the buggy, but you don't need one to drive it."

The horse slowed to a gentle trot, making Hunter feel better about it. Once he steadied his pace, things seemed fine and he relaxed a little, the tension in his shoulders burning.

The jingling of the bells on the harness filled the cold air, the horse blowing out rolling puffs of icy air from his nostrils.

"Don't you get cold riding in this all winter?" he asked.

She pulled a lap quilt from under the seat. "That is why we keep these in here; would you like to share it?"

He nodded, a smile curving his lips.

She spread the lap quilt between them, and it sent a surge of warmth through him, though he knew it had nothing to do with the quilt. He would love to be alone for such a ride with her; it would be romantic to have her lay her head on his shoulder as he drove the buggy over snowy paths, the jingle bells mesmerizing them with a romance that was unlike any he'd ever experienced. Even with their kids and Becca in the back seat of the buggy, it was still plenty romantic.

"Make the horse go faster, Daddy," Raegan called from the back seat of the open buggy.

"You let me get used to him first, Pumpkin," he said.

He leaned in toward Noel. "I'm a little nervous of the traffic going around us."

"Keep a steady tension on both leads, and let the horse do the driving; Old Yeller knows the way."

Hunter flashed Noel a smile. "You do know Old Yeller was a dog, don't you?"

She laughed. "Of course, I do; another wonderful book I read."

He winked at her and smiled. "You seem to like those classics, don't you?"

She nodded, keeping her hand on his. He liked the closeness of the front seat of the buggy, the larger, curved back seat big enough to accommodate four.

"How many times do you want to go around?" he asked. "It's getting late, and I'm sure my pop will be done with bingo soon."

"Once more?" she asked with a warm smile.

How could he resist that smile?

He nodded. "This is the most fun I've had in a while," he admitted.

"Me too," she said, barely above a whisper.

RAEGAN skipped alongside her dad as they walked up into the pavilion to fetch her grandpa. "Can we do that again, Daddy?"

"I don't see why not, but I'll have to ask Mrs. Fisher."

His heart thumped again; it was the first he'd thought of Noel as being a *Missus*. He didn't know why, but it almost bothered him. It wasn't like he wasn't married before too, but he wondered if she was over her husband's death yet. He wasn't over Kate, and he wasn't sure if he ever would be, and no one could ever take her place in his heart, but he was ready to move on. Tonight proved that for him. He wondered how Noel felt about her husband; was she ready to move on yet?

Raegan ran up to her grandpa and jumped up and down. "Poppy, did you see us taking a carriage ride in my new sister's buggy?"

His dad looked at him and smiled. "Buggy ride? New sister?"

Hunter put a hand up to stop his comments. "I'll explain it all later."

"Yes, Poppy, Gabby is my best friend and we're going to be sisters!"

Hunter picked up his daughter. "What makes you think she's going to be your sister just because you two are friends?"

"Because Gabby told me we can be secret sisters—that means we give each other presents at Christmas!"

Hunter let out his breath with a whoosh. "Whew! Rae, you're taking years off your daddy's life with the grownup ways you talk sometimes. I'm glad you're going to be secret sisters with Gabby."

"We have to go shopping, Daddy, so I can get stuff to make a present."

"Don't you mean, you want to buy her a present?" he asked.

"No! Silly Daddy! Gabby said the rules are you have to make something for your secret sister."

"Oh, so there's *rules* for being a secret sister?"

She nodded. "She told me I could make her something, and she's making me something."

"Did she give you any ideas of what she wants?"

Another shake of her head. "Nope! She said it has to be a surprise."

"Would you like to make her something in the woodshop? I can help you."

She nodded, smiled and threw her arms around him in a big hug. "I knew you'd understand, Daddy."

I wish I did. I suppose I should be thankful she didn't mean the two of them were real sisters. But would that be so bad?

"Let's get you home, kiddo, you know it's almost eight o'clock and it's a school night, and we still have to come back tomorrow night and Friday after school to set up for the parade. It's going to be a busy week."

"Are we going to take another buggy ride with Gabby?"

"I'll ask her mommy, but first, I want to go check on my entry for the silent auction. I'm kind of interested in seeing how much it will bring in for the cause."

He put Raegan down and let her run ahead.

"I take it you had a good evening with that beautiful Amish woman," his dad said, once Raegan was out of earshot.

"Hey, Squirt, you can't get on Santa's sleigh." He chuckled and turned his attention back to his father. "Yes, I did have a wonderful time, but I don't want to read too much into it."

"Do you like her? She looked like she was interested in you."

"Yes, Pop, I like her, and I'd like to ask her out, but I'm just not sure how things would go; we are from two different cultures."

"Aw, who cares about that?" his dad asked, swiping his hand at the air. "Life is too short to worry about that stuff; you know better than others how quickly you can lose someone. It was like that with your mother and me; we lived each day together as if it could be our last. It made for a wonderful happy marriage and I miss her like crazy."

"I miss Kate that way too, Pop; I guess it scares me to think I could lose someone like that again."

"Son, you can't worry your whole life away; if you like her, then take the chance. You can't lose something you never had, and if you don't try then you'll never know what it's like to love again. You have a lot of years ahead of you; no one knew Kate would have an aneurysm. Life is unpredictable—go with it and live it as fully as possible. They say life is for the living; you're alive, so enjoy it without worry and without guilt."

"Thanks, Pop, that's good advice; how'd you get to be so wise?"

"Unfortunately, it comes with age," he said with a chuckle. "Boy, if I'd known what I know now when I was younger, I might have been too dangerous for my own good."

Hunter laughed. "I think I believe you."

When they caught up to Raegan, she was standing in front of the table with his dollhouse on it. The signup sheet was on a clipboard in front of it. He picked it up and chuckled, his heart skipping a beat.

"What's so funny, Son?"

He showed his dad the paper. Noel had put in a bid of three dozen gingerbread cookies.

"You can't pass up that bid," his dad said, smiling. "That woman is sweet on you."

Hunter smiled. "You really think so?"

"A woman doesn't make an offer like that unless she's serious."

"It's funny, but I'd had the same exact thought earlier."

His dad sucked in a breath, his eyes wide. "It's fate, Son; don't miss this opportunity."

"You really believe in all that stuff?"

"Absolutely! God dropped that one in your lap—don't let it go—don't let *her* go. She's a keeper!"

The old man winked at him and nudged him with his elbow.

"I'll figure out what I'm going to do tomorrow; right now, I've got a kid who's had too much sugar tonight, and I'm not sure how I'm going to get her to settle down."

All the way home, Hunter couldn't take his mind off Noel. He hadn't felt this alive since Kate was still with him.

Once they were home, he put on a pot of coffee while he waited for Raegan to put her PJ's on and brush her teeth.

"I'm ready, Daddy and Poppy!" she called from her room.

They went into her room and she jumped under the covers. He pulled it up to her neck and tucked it in around her. "Let's get you tucked in snug as a bug in a rug because it is supposed to get really cold tonight."

"Is it going to snow some more? Maybe we'll have a snow-day!"

He laughed at his daughter's comment. "I don't think we're in for a blizzard tonight, so don't get your hopes up. Besides, I thought you liked school."

"I do, Daddy, but I want Christmas to hurry up and get here too, and when I get out of school for winter break, then it will be almost Christmas."

Hunter put a hand under her pillow and pulled out the envelope. "I thought you'd be more excited about the visit from the Tooth Fairy tonight."

She squealed and grabbed the envelope. "I forgot all about the Tooth Fairy!"

She pushed it back under her pillow and smiled. It almost broke his heart wishing her mom could see her now, but he prayed she was able to watch over Raegan from Heaven. She'd be so proud.

Her grandpa sat on the opposite side of the bed from her dad, and the two men joined hands with Raegan.

She closed her eyes, and Hunter began his prayer.

"God bless mommy in Heaven," Raegan added. "And please let Gabby be my real sister; she said she would share her mommy with me and I need a new mommy. That is what I want more than anything for Christmas."

Hunter found it difficult to breathe; he had no idea his daughter wanted a mother as badly as she did.

"God bless Daddy and Poppy, and please help me stay awake so I can see the Tooth Fairy. Amen"

Hunter chuckled. "That's quite a long list for God tonight, Pumpkin." He kissed her cheek and gave her a big bear hug like he did every night. "I love you. Sweet dreams."

"I love you too Daddy, and I love you too Poppy."

After a kiss from her grandpa, Hunter turned out the light, thinking he needed a cup of strong coffee.

His dad patted him on the shoulder and chuckled. "Son, you're in big trouble if you don't make that pretty little Amish woman your wife and give that child a mommy for Christmas!"

That was a pretty tall order in such a short time.

CHAPTER ELEVEN

ALICE parker approached Hunter's truck with her usual enthusiasm that he always tried so hard to ignore; today, he'd been so deep in thought, she'd caught him off guard. She startled him so much he nearly dumped his coffee in his lap. Thankful for the new thermal cup he'd gotten that came with a non-spill lid, he turned to her, his jaw dropping open, and he couldn't find his voice.

She smiled brightly, her hair at least three inches lower on her head than usual, and her face was almost completely devoid of makeup. Her dress was conservative; it covered her top, and it draped just over her knees.

"I'm sorry if I came across as rude to you last night," she said. "But you actually made me think last night. And I didn't mean to offend your wife; she's really very lovely, although I have to admit I envy her."

Hunter sighed; he had to tell her the truth even if it caused her to go back to being obnoxious. He hated to do it because she was actually being nice. He cleared his throat; it was now or never. "She's not really my wife," he said. "I didn't marry her yesterday, but you shouldn't envy her, no matter what."

Alice leaned onto his truck. "I guess I don't blame you for fibbing to me; I guess I have been coming on really strong, and I'm sorry."

Wow! I got an apology out of her. Wait till Holly hears about this.

She furrowed her brow. "Tell me honestly what it is I'm doing wrong."

"You *really* want my honest opinion?" Hunter asked. "I don't want you keying up my truck or anything!"

She giggled nervously. "I would never do that."

Somehow, I doubt that, but here goes a good dose of honesty.

"Today, you look very lovely," he said. "But, you've only got it half-right. Your dress is very conservative and *proper;* the *right man* will appreciate that. Now, all you have to do is lose the *desperate, drama queen* attitude and you'll find a good man—one who won't treat you like the last one did."

"But I'm the PTA president," she said. "People *expect* me to be a mean, drama queen. If I'm nice it'll ruin my reputation."

He threw his hands up in mock-defeat. "Okay, but I thought you wanted my advice."

"Oh, I do," she said scrunching her face up into a desperate smile. "But can't I be both?"

Hunter cinched his brow and narrowed his eyes. "No! Not if you ever want to date again—which I suspect you do.'

"I was hoping to date *you,* Mr. Darcy." She fluttered her lashes at him and it made him cringe.

She was a beautiful woman, but God had a lot of work to do on her before she'd be ready to date; he couldn't tell her that. He'd said too much already.

"I'm sorry, but I'm interested in someone else."

She rolled her eyes. "That Amish woman?"

He pointed at her. "See, that's what I'm talking about; be nice—if you want to catch a nice man, you've got to be nice."

"Thank you, Mr. Darcy," she said. "I wish you luck with the Amish woman; she's very pretty."

He smiled. "I think so. Thank you, *Alice;* I wish the best for you, too."

HUNTER left the car-line feeling a lot lighter than he had since school started; Alice had become a thorn in his side, and now, it was possible she could end up being someone he wouldn't feel the need to avoid. It was a liberating feeling to know he could get in line for drop off and pickup, and not be cornered by her every time.

His only focus now that Raegan was at school was to go to Noel to see if her offer to help him was a sincere one. He parked his truck in front of **Bäckerei Noel** and put a quarter in the meter. Then he lifted the box containing the dollhouse and went to the door. Holding it with one arm and balancing it against his chest, he managed to get the door. Noel rushed to the door; although she didn't get there in time, she was still able to hold it open so he could get inside. Snow was coming down in wet clumps, and he was worried the contents would get soaked.

He stepped inside and breathed in deep; he could sure get used to the aroma of fresh baked bread and cinnamon. Noel wiped her hands on her apron and pushed nervously at stray brown curls that fell from her *kapp*.

Her eyes lit up when her gaze focused on the large box he'd carried inside; it was just the reaction he was hoping for.

"What's in the box?" she asked, her smile wider than a kid's at Christmas.

"It's the dollhouse you bid on—well not the same one—it's a duplicate from my shop."

"I know my bid did not win that dollhouse!" she said, suppressing a smile.

He smiled. "No, but your offer for three dozen gingerbread cookies made me think we could make a trade."

"I'm not so sure that's a fair trade, Mr. Darcy," she said.

"Please call me Hunter," he said. "I probably wouldn't argue with you about it being a fair trade, but I'm a desperate man, so at this point, those cookies are priceless!"

She laughed. "That much, huh?"

"I made a dozen of these dollhouses hoping to sell them for the holidays and I have two left. With it being so close to Christmas, I'll probably only sell one more, but this one seems to have Gabby's name on it. Even if you won't help me, I want her to have it."

"That's more than generous, *Hunter,*" she said, her eyes cast downward.

"I give you my word that if you trade me the cookies, I'll be honest and let everyone know where I got the cookies; they won't be able to deny they're homemade, but I'll give you the credit. I'm sure it'll help you with last-minute sales for Christmas."

"*Danki,* I appreciate that," Noel said. "How can I say no when I can see how much those cookies mean to you?"

He shook his head. "No, my daughter means that much to me."

"It's nice to see a *vadder* so caring for his *dochder.*"

He could see pain in her eyes; she had to have been thinking of her own daughter. Being without her father had to be just as tough on her as being without a mother was for Raegan.

"Gabby must miss her dad."

"Thankfully, she was too young to remember when he left," she said.

"Left?"

She kept her eyes to the floor. "He ran off with a wealthy *English* woman; he divorced me, so he could marry her."

Hunter's heart flip-flopped in his chest; no wonder she didn't want to be any part of his deception about the cookies.

"I'm sorry he did that to you; I don't believe in divorce," he said. "He obviously didn't know what he was giving up when he let you go."

She lifted her gaze and her breath hitched. *"Danki,* for your kind words."

He held fast to the dollhouse, knowing if he put it down he might not be able to control the urge to pull her into his arms and kiss her. Whatever that man must have put her through, she didn't deserve it. What a jerk!

"Those aren't just words, Noel, I meant every one of them."

"He brought shame to me and Gabby," she said. "I wasn't shunned outright, but the community turned their backs on me, and so I sold the farm that my parents passed down to us when we got married, and I bought this building for my bakery—but also because it had living space above the store. I never imagined I would have to make a living upstairs, but I've managed to make it a home."

He toyed with the idea of putting the box down and rescuing her from her husband's shame, but he thought better of it. The last thing she needed was a man she referred to as an *Englisher* to make a pass at her after all she'd been put through by a husband who chose to be an *Englisher,* rather than fulfill his marriage commitment to her.

"I bought my shop for the same reason. I had renovated the space above it and had intended to rent it out. But it turned out that God had other plans for that space. When my wife died suddenly of an aneurysm, I was lost and never wanted to move, but as the days passed and the walls began to close in on me with memories, I put the house up for sale and made the move into town."

"I'm sorry for your loss," she said, her eyes still cast to the floor.

That was it; he couldn't help himself even another second. He set the dollhouse down and closed the space between them, the jingling of the bells on the door breaking the spell between them. He jolted back a step when Gabby came bouncing into the lobby of the bakery with Becca on her heels.

"Hello, Daddy!" she said.

His heart nearly stopped beating; was that another *little girl thing* that he didn't understand, or did she think he was her father?"

"Gabby, what did you call him?" Noel asked.

She looked up at him with wide blue eyes that matched her mother's.

"Raegan told me your name was *Daddy,* and I think that's a nice name."

"That's what Raegan tells me." He smiled and waved a hand to Noel. "I don't mind, if you don't."

She chuckled lightly and shrugged; it seemed that God was turning them into a ready-made family—at the speed of light!

Becca took Gabby upstairs to work on her lessons, and Hunter was relieved to get a break from the constant jolts to his heart she kept doling out. It wasn't like she was saying anything that wasn't already rolling around his head, but it was another thing to have it said out loud. If he didn't know better, he'd swear that Noel was enjoying every bit of it; the smile on her face was giving her away. Truth was, he liked it too, even if it did make his heart skip a beat.

The jingle bells on the door caused him to turn around again. "I'm so glad I caught the two of you together!" Brenda said.

Together? What?

She stomped the snow off her boots onto the rug in front of the door.

"The two of you have been requested to be in the live Nativity tonight! Everyone agrees that the two of you are such a cute couple, you've just got to say yes!"

Cute couple? I wish my heart rate would have a chance to slow down.

Hunter smiled and looked toward Noel. "I'm game if you are."

She nodded, biting her lip. "Alright, I can do it; I also have the cake I promised you for the Cake-Walk booth in the pavilion tonight."

"I'm so glad," she said, turning her attention on Hunter.

He couldn't take his eyes off Noel; he watched her remove a Santa cake from the glass case and put it in a pink box. She tied ribbon around it and then handed it to Brenda, who seemed to be patiently waiting for him to give her his full attention.

"I was hoping I could talk you into entering the bachelor auction on Friday," Brenda said, holding both her hands up and crossing her fingers.

He shot a sideways glance in Noel's direction, who had a hand over her mouth trying to suppress giggles.

"What is so funny?" he asked. "You don't think I'd bring in the money?"

She nodded. "I'm sure you'll get the highest bid."

Is she planning on bidding? Hmm…if so, I'll be more than happy to enter!

"Is that a *yes?*" Brenda asked.

He puffed up his chest and stood tall, jutting out his chin. "I believe it is."

Wait! That wasn't my voice! Can I take it back?

There was that thumping again; his heart was going to pop right out of his chest if he didn't stop putting his foot in his mouth.

Brenda snickered. "I believe my work here is done! I'll let you two get back to whatever it was I interrupted." She winked and smiled before leaving the bakery.

CHAPTER TWELVE

HUNTER put a hand over his chest; if he was going to continue to keep this woman's company, he'd better get used to the unusual beatings of his heart.

"Shall we get to work?" Noel asked, catching him off guard.

"Work?"

She pointed to the kitchen. "Baking those three dozen gingerbread cookies you need for Raegan's class party tomorrow."

"Oh, well I hadn't planned on…"

"You didn't expect *me* to bake them by myself, did you?"

He forced a smile; that was exactly what he'd planned on.

"I promised to teach you how to bake those cookies and that's what I intend to do; I want you to be able to take pride in the cookies when you take them to the party."

He clapped his hands and rubbed them together. "Alright, I'm ready."

He took off his coat and followed her into the kitchen. "Where do I start?"

She pointed to the sink at the back wall.

He scrunched his brow and chuckled. "You want me to wash dishes?"

She giggled. "I want you to wash your hands and then put on an apron."

He chuckled. "I'll wash my hands, but I draw a line at putting on an apron."

She folded her arms and tapped her foot on the floor. Kate used to do that to him; he thought it was cute.

He threw his hands up defensively. "Okay, okay, I'll put on the apron."

He rolled up the sleeves of his blue striped dress shirt and turned on the faucet to wash his hands. Behind him, Noel clanked stainless-steel bowls and utensils as she gathered the things needed to make the cookies. Happy to find a plain white apron amongst the frilly ones, Hunter tucked the loop around his neck and tied it at his waist. He smoothed down the front and went over to the long, stainless-steel counter where Noel had everything ready.

He picked up the measuring spoons and eyed them. "These are a little small, don't you think?"

"They're the same size as the ones you used when you baked your cookies, aren't they?" she asked.

He shook his head.

Noel held up the measuring cup. "Did you use one of these to measure the flour?"

Another shake of his head.

"Nope; coffee cup!"

She snickered. "I'm beginning to see that we need to start from the very beginning and I need to teach you the importance of proper measuring first."

He waved a hand in the air. "I've watched all those cooking shows and those professional chefs don't measure anything. They put in a dash of this and a handful of that; I've never seen them use these fancy spoons or a measuring cup. They say a cup of something, but they have it in a bowl, or a little dish."

"I've seen some of those shows too, and I'm telling you those little bowls are for show; they've already measured the ingredients and put them into the little bowls, so everything looks pretty for the program."

He stared blankly at her.

"I have Mennonite cousins, and they have TV; that's how I know."

He nodded and smiled, picking up the bottle of ginger. He opened the lid and sniffed it. "I always liked the smell of these spices; it reminds me of my mom. She used to bake a lot. My Kate baked a little too."

He wasn't sure why he brought up Kate; he supposed he felt a little awkward and didn't know how to fill the silence.

"It's alright to talk about her; I don't mind," Noel said. "I can tell you're a man who loves very deeply."

He nodded. *She gets me!*

She began her lesson, explaining each of the utensils and introducing all the spices and told him about their role in the process. Who knew baking required so much knowledge? If you'd have asked him even an hour ago, he'd warn you that baking wasn't easy, but he'd have never guessed it was this complex. He assumed baking was like gardening—you either had a *green thumb* or you didn't.

Obviously, it wasn't that cut and dry.

She'd gotten out two mixing bowls, so he could mimic her every move. He was a hands-on kind of guy, so this method of teaching was perfect for him. Turns out, it was important to melt the butter—who knew? He cracked his egg into a smaller bowl—at Noel's suggestion. She was right about that too!

Eggshells were not that easy to retrieve from the bowl, but he managed with a little help from his teacher. The molasses, he discovered, was a lot easier to remove from the cup if the measuring cup was sprayed with cooking spray first. It was really fascinating for him to learn a few new tricks. Maybe there was something to this baking thing; it was actually relaxing—and fun. He packed the brown sugar into the smaller measuring cup and dropped it into the bowl. Using a stand mixer, they took turns putting their stainless-steel bowls under it, and they had the beginnings of cookie dough.

Little bits of the video came to mind, and although her methods were a little different, they'd accomplished the same results so far. Next, she grabbed two more mixing bowls from the bottom shelf of the open counter and placed one in front of him.

"Now we have to mix the dry ingredients." She handed him a sifter.

He chuckled.

"What's so funny about the sifter? If you don't sift your flour, your dough could be lumpy."

"When I made my cookies, I used my bacon screen because I didn't have a sifter and it made an awful mess."

She laughed. "I'd sure like to know how you made those cookies; they would come in handy for keeping my gingerbread houses longer into the season. I have to time them just right, so they don't spoil before Christmas."

"I don't think I could repeat that process if my life depended on it—I have no idea how I did it!"

They sifted the spices, measuring them each just right, and he could see already he'd put too much in. His second batch had certainly smelled nice, but he supposed that was because he'd put so much spice in them.

Next, they combined the dry and wet ingredients together and put them under the mixer, using what Noel explained to him was a dough hook.

"Now the dough has to be refrigerated for three hours, but I made a large batch of dough when I got up this morning."

"How did you know I was going to show up here?"

She giggled. "I figured you would eventually to get your cookies, but I'm happy you came in and decided to bake with me. I'll use the dough we made just now for a batch to fill an order I have coming in for pickup later today."

He chuckled. "You trust my batch?"

She bit her lip to keep from smiling and nodded. "I walked you through it, so it will be fine. Separate your dough into three sections of the same amount and roll them into balls."

She ripped sheets of plastic wrap and placed the squares onto the counter, instructing him to put each of his dough balls onto one square. Then they wrapped them and flattened them to about two inches thick. After they placed the dough in the large refrigerator, she loaded up his arms with cold dough balls she'd made earlier.

They placed them on the counter and cleared the dishes. "I didn't use this many dishes to make my cookies!"

She smiled. "If you had made them the right way, you would have used more dishes."

She finished wiping down the counter and then reached for two rolling pins and the bag of flour. Then she opened one of the many drawers under the counter and pulled out two gingerbread cookie cutters—one male and one female. A burst of laughter escaped him before he could stop it.

She paused and stared at him, trying not to laugh.

He shook his head. "You don't want to know where I got my cookie cutter; I'm too ashamed to tell anyone."

She gasped. "Please don't tell me you found it in the trash or something."

He threw his head back and laughed. "Is that the sort of things that women think of men?"

She narrowed her eyes. "I've heard of the *ten-second-rule!*"

He rolled his eyes, avoiding her. "As long as no critter gets to it before I do, I'm fine with it!"

"Oh no; you're kidding, aren't you?"

"I'm a country boy—used to sleeping under the stars and fishing for my dinner. You sometimes end up with ants getting into your food. It won't hurt you; it's protein!"

"Yuck!"

He snickered. "I'm kidding with you; even though I'm an outdoor kind of guy, I'm not a fan of bugs—except fireflies."

"I used to catch them when I was young," she said.

"I just caught a jar-full this past summer when Raegan and I went camping at the state park."

Her eyes lit up. "I've never been camping before."

"Oh, you'd love it; maybe we'll have to plan a trip this summer."

He hadn't meant to make plans like that; he was getting way ahead of himself again.

"I'd like that."

Her comment surprised him.

The jingling of the bells on the front door of the bakery broke the spell between them.

"Start rolling out the dough while I take care of the customer."

Thinking he could impress her and have his cookies cut out before she returned, he put the dough on the flour-dusted counter and put the rolling pin down on it. It was stiff and hard to push. He rolled a couple of times trying to flatten it, but the dough stuck to the rolling pin on both sides. Oh no, she was going to laugh at him again.

Giggling from the front of the bakery made him forget all about the sticky dough. His ears perked up and he moved closer to the entryway, so he could eavesdrop.

Jack Baker smiled at Noel. "You know I only come in here because you're sweeter than your treats."

Was that supposed to be a compliment? Sounded more like a put-down of her baked-goods.

She giggled.

Does she like him?

"I'm going to be in the bachelor auction on Friday night," he said. "I hope you'll be there, so you can bid on me."

Hunter popped his head out from around the corner. "Hey, Jack, what's up?"

His jaw dropped open. "What are you doing here with my girl?"

Hunter's eyes widened, and he chuckled. "Your girl? Last night she agreed to be my wife, buddy, so you're too late."

Jack turned to Noel, his brow cinched. "Tell me that's not true."

Hunter closed the space between them and put his arm around her, his arm tingling from the excitement of it. "Does that answer your question?"

He put his hands up. "I'm sorry, Dude, I didn't mean to crunch in on your territory."

Hunter put on his best stern look—the one that usually worked on Reagan.

"I'll forgive you since you didn't know, but don't let it happen again," he said. "And pass the word around; I don't want anyone else at the factory trying to put the moves on my fiancée."

Maybe that was taking it a bit too far; she's never going to get another date again with me saying that—not that I want her to. Oh no! Do I love her already?

Jack planted his hands on his hips and jutted out his chin. "I don't see a ring on her finger!"

Are you really going to take it that far, buddy? What are we, in high school?

"The Amish don't wear rings," Noel said.

Hunter threw up his free arm toward Jack. "Well, there you have it; the Amish don't wear—huh? What?" he asked her, dumbfounded. "Really?" he shot a sideways glance at her and then shook his head furiously. "Doesn't matter; I'm getting her one anyway!"

Jack chuckled. "I'll believe that when I see it. Can I get my sister's order, so I can get out of here? I think the lies in this place are pretty thick." He waved at the air as if to demonstrate swatting at *flies*.

Hunter removed his arm from around Noel and leaned against the wall, arms folded, but overlooking the transaction between her and Jack. His arm still tingled from having it around her, and he wished it could have been a real hug.

Once Jack left the bakery, Noel turned around and leaned her back against the front counter and stared at him. "Why did you say all that?"

Hunter smiled. "You seemed like you needed rescuing!"

He went back to the kitchen and pointed to rolling pin. "Sort of like I do right now! How do I get that dough unstuck from that thing without ruining it?"

She suppressed a giggle. "You have to dust it with flour."

She carefully peeled away the sticky dough, rubbing a little flour on the rolling pin as she did. Then she motioned for him to come over to her. "You've managed to press a hole in the middle, while the sides are too thick; put your hands over mine, so you can feel the amount of pressure I use."

He stood behind her, very aware of how short and dainty she was when he wrapped his arms around her and placed his hands over hers. A bolt of tingling energy shot up his arms and traveled to his toes. His breathing hitched when he bent over her shoulder; he wanted to bury his face in her neck and get lost in kisses with her, but he knew better than to overstep his boundaries where she was concerned. He would wait for permission for such boldness; would she give it freely?

Her breath hitched when his cheek brushed hers and she paused.

He turned his face toward hers, brushing his lips across her cheek, but he didn't kiss her. He stopped at her temple; he couldn't help but breathe her in. A mixture of spices and lilac tickled his senses; he closed his eyes and paused there.

The jingling of the bells on the front door broke the spell between them once more. She straightened her back and he bolted upright.

"Hey, Son," his father said from the lobby. "I didn't know where you were; I didn't know you had a date with this lovely woman."

There goes that heart-thumping again! Great timing, Pop!

"It's not a date, Pop," he said, flashing his dad a warning look.

The gleam in the old man's eyes told him he was in for more of the same.

"She's teaching me how to bake gingerbread cookies, so I can make the ones I need for Rae's class."

"I think the aroma of fresh coffee and cinnamon bread brought me over here. I've got Ira minding the store, so I could step out and enjoy the snow for a few minutes while I walked across the park to follow my nose; it led me here!"

"Would you like to sit and have some coffee to warm you up?" Noel asked. "How do you take it, Sir?"

"Sir?" he asked as he sat at a table in front of the window. "From the looks of your cooking lesson, young lady, you better get used to calling me *Pop!*"

Her cheeks turned pink and she smiled shyly. "Okay, *Pop,*" she said, straightening her back. "How do you take your coffee? I better learn that if the two of you are going to become regular furniture in here."

"Black, two sugars!" he said, taking his coat off.

He wasn't planning on leaving; he was going to enjoy the show while his son squirmed and denied his feelings for Noel.

CHAPTER THIRTEEN

NOEL removed her *Mary* costume and put it in the trunk next to Hunter's costume. Since his father had hung around while they cut and baked the first batch of cookies she hadn't had much of a chance to talk to him. She'd had a good laugh when Hunter had surprised himself at how well he could now bake—with her help, of course. There hadn't been another encounter between them, and she had hoped he'd kiss her, but they'd been interrupted too many times. She had to wonder if it was for the best; were they moving too fast? Or perhaps it was all to make her want it even more.

She reasoned with herself that they were too old to draw things out the way they had when they were younger. Life was too short to wait for something if you felt strongly enough about it, and she was grateful that his father seemed to be onboard with it. Would his sister and brother agree if they should meet? Surely, if they began to date—or something more serious, she would meet his siblings, and she worried about their approval of her. She'd been so untrusting of the *English* because of what her husband had done to her, but now, she had to believe they weren't all like Silas had turned out to be.

She shivered, and her teeth chattered. The long robes of her costume had kept her warm for the past hour, and now she felt the chill blow right up her dress.

Hunter removed his jacket and draped it over her.

She shrugged it away.

"You put that coat back on, Hunter; you'll catch cold. It can't be more than thirty degrees, and that wind blows right through you."

"Which is exactly why you need to keep this around you; I can't imagine how cold your legs must be. Aren't you *allowed* to wear pants even in the winter?"

She hadn't really thought about what she was *allowed* to do since she was young and wanting to try new things out on her *Rumspringa,* but she'd given that up to marry Silas. She supposed now that she wasn't part of the community any longer, it suddenly seemed silly that she kept the traditions. She was free to do anything she wanted—including wearing a pair of jeans and a sweater.

"I have leggings, but didn't think it would be that cold tonight."

She relaxed beneath the warmth of his jacket that still held his body heat.

"Since the girls are inside with Becca and your Pop, would you like to get some hot cocoa and take the buggy around the block once or twice?"

Hunter laughed. "He's your Pop now too, remember?"

"He wasn't serious, was he?"

"Oh, yeah! Once that man gets something in his head, it's tough to break him from it."

He took her arm and tucked it into the crook of his arm and they walked toward her buggy, which was parked at the end of Candy Cane Lane. Every year, the city workers put

Christmas-related signs up in the town square and in the large park in the center of the downtown area. It made it almost seem like a Christmas town. She loved the hometown feeling.

Snow drifted onto her lashes and she blinked it away.

"With all the decorations and snow falling, it sort of feels like we live in a snow globe," he said with a chuckle.

"*Jah,* it does."

They stopped at a booth along the path and ordered two hot cocoas.

When they reached her buggy, he assisted her up into it, walked over and patted the horse, and then climbed in beside her. She shrugged out of his coat after tucking a lap quilt around her legs, but he put it back around her.

"You keep that on until you get warmed up; I'm fine—I've got this ugly Santa sweater that my sister bought for me last Christmas."

"You don't like the gift, but you wear it anyway; that's a very admirable quality in a man."

He tapped on the reins and set the horse at a slow canter—just enough to get the bells jingling. He was more confident tonight and it made her smile; she could get used to having him drive. Or perhaps she might consider taking a ride in his shiny black truck.

"Let me explain," Hunter said. "Every year, for the past ten years or so, Holly and I started a new tradition of seeing who could find the ugliest Christmas sweater, and of course we would have Pop judge the sweaters. I got this one last year with the floppy Santa hat hanging off the front of it. I have to wear it until the new one arrives."

"I'm guessing she won last year," Noel said with a giggle. "This is pretty bad."

"Oh no! I won!"

She laughed. "I'm afraid to ask how bad hers was."

"Picture a sweater with a moose head hanging off the front with a trophy plaque behind it—kind of like the ones you hang on a wall. The antlers stuck out so far she couldn't close her coat over it," he said, demonstrating how far out the sweater stuck out. "But wait! It gets worse than that."

She put her hand to her mouth to cover the gasp. "How much worse could that possibly get?"

He laughed so hard he had to wait a minute before his laughter slowed so he could tell her. She really liked his laugh.

"Hanging from the antlers were jingle bells, so when she walked, it jingled!"

He busted out laughing again, and she joined him, unable to hold it in any longer. Oh, her stomach hurt she was laughing so hard. She couldn't remember the last time she laughed that much. She loved that he made her laugh.

"I'd have to agree that you won that one!" Noel said.

He laughed some more, and she couldn't help but giggle with him.

"What about your brother? Is he younger or older?"

Hunter cleared his throat. "Hayden is younger, and very serious—too serious. He never wanted in on the ugly sweater thing. Holly got him one a few years back, but he refused to wear it. He's the baby of the family and always thinks he has to prove himself. He's made a good life for himself as an architect. I always told him that, with his drawing skills and my wood skills, we could go into business together building houses. He's ending an apprenticeship in two weeks, and he's supposed to come with Holly for a week after Christmas, so we'll see how that goes."

"It sounds as if he needs a family visit; perhaps you should get him a nice sweater."

"I hadn't thought of that; he does wear those sweater-vests—like a college professor!"

"You could try Nathan's Men's Shoppe on the other side of the square," she suggested.

"Great idea, thank you," he said. "What about you? Do you have family besides Becca?"

"I have one older brother, Hiram, and he hasn't talked to me since the trouble with Silas. I'm almost thankful both my parents passed away before he divorced me; I wouldn't have been able to bear it if they had shunned me. They had Hiram and me when they were too old to have children, and were more like grandparents than parents. They lived long enough to see Gabby born, but died within a few days of each other. My *Vadder* went first, and my *mudder* couldn't live without him."

Hunter put a hand over hers. "I'm so sorry you don't have any family."

She lifted her chin. "I have Becca; without her staying by my side in all of this, I probably wouldn't have gotten through it. She's almost like a sister—we have always been close."

"Raegan is going to be upset with me, but I'm afraid we don't have time for a buggy ride tonight; it's late and she's going to be a mess in the morning," he said. "All this activity for the Twelve Days of Christmas and Festival of Lights they have going on every night has worn her out. It won't be so bad after tomorrow since it's her last day of school, but we have to get through tomorrow with as few tears as possible, and that means getting home and putting her to bed."

"If you're going to the moonlight skating party on Goose Pond on Saturday night, perhaps we can take a buggy ride after," Noel suggested.

"Yes, we'll be there; I got her a new pair of skates for that party last year and she needs to finish breaking them in this year!"

She smiled. "I'll see you in the morning, so we can get those cookies decorated for the party," she said, wishing he would kiss her goodnight.

He paused before hopping out of the buggy, and she detected a hint of reluctance in his eyes; was it possible he wanted to kiss her just as badly as she wanted him to?

HUNTER left the car line with no harassment from Alice; in fact, she hadn't even been there. Relieved he'd avoided her the last day of school before break, he prayed he could do the same during the Christmas party.

Now, all he had on his mind was getting over to the bakery, so he could ice the cookies he helped Noel bake. He never thought he'd like to bake cookies, but being near her made it fun. He couldn't wait to see her; he'd barely slept all night thinking about her. He almost felt as giddy as a teenager looking forward to his first date. Only this was different; it was serious and grownup. He could see himself wanting a lifetime with Noel. He knew it was strange; they barely knew each other, but for some reason, it was if he always knew her.

NOEL readied herself for the party while Becca finished boxing up all the cookies. She was a little unsure of herself and decided that although she would wear her hair up, she would leave her *kapp* at home, along with her apron.

Her plain dress would make her look a little more *Mennonite,* and she'd made up her mind to stand out as least as possible; the last thing she wanted to do was to embarrass Hunter or Raegan. She was certain Gabby would not argue with her about leaving her own things behind, as she often complained about the encumbrance of the apron and *kapp.* She'd struggled all this time with wondering if raising Gabby as Amish was the best thing for her, and now she felt as if she'd gotten her answer. She wanted more than anything to fit in, and she wanted the same for her daughter. Hunter had been kind enough to lend her an outfit for Gabby after she'd asked him. It was only for one afternoon, and Gabby would think it was fun playing dress-up.

She looked one last time in the mirror, wondering what it would be like to marry an *Englisher.* Surely, Hunter wasn't that serious about her, was he?

Lord, guard my heart, and don't let me make a fool of myself with Hunter. I really care for him—I might even love him!

She went into the other room to see how Gabby was coming along with the borrowed outfit. Her breath nearly caught in her throat when she saw her child looking—*English.*

"How do I look, *Mamm?"*

"Ach, you look very beautiful. Do you like Raegan's clothes?"

"Jah, I want to wear them all the time."

"You don't like wearing your dresses?"

She shook her head. "No, I get too cold, even with my leggings. I want to wear pants like Raegan does."

She supposed she hadn't realized that she'd never given her child a voice in how they would live outside of the community. She'd asked several times why they were different from the *Englishers,* but she'd never been able to answer her daughter.

Looking at Gabby now, she didn't see a difference at all.

HUNTER pulled up to the bakery and hopped out to help Noel with the boxes of cookies.

One look at her and his heart started that fluttering again. She certainly took his breath away. Her hair fell against her cheeks in wispy, auburn ringlets, her blue eyes matching her light blue floral dress—minus the apron. He didn't think he'd seen her yet without an apron, but he was happy to now. She didn't look *English,* but he didn't want her to; she was beautiful just the way she was.

"Daddy!" Gabby said, running toward him. He scooped her up and hugged her, and it was as natural as if she was his own daughter.

Once everyone was secure in his truck, they headed for the school that was less than a mile away.

He was tempted to hold Noel's hand as they entered the school, but he didn't want to push his luck with her; most of all, he didn't want to embarrass her. She'd agreed to go with him when he'd asked her to, and he was proud and happy she'd said yes.

They entered the classroom and Raegan spotted them; her face lit up when she saw Gabby there. She ran up and gave him a quick hug and then grabbed Gabby by the hand and led her over to Jenna Parker.

"I told you my sister was coming to the party!" Raegan said to her.

"Can I sit with you?" Jenna asked.

Both girls smiled and invited her to sit with them, and Hunter let out his breath with a whoosh. The last thing he wanted was for Raegan to alienate her classmates because of Gabby's presence at the party. He rested assured that his gentle teachings on how to treat others had blossomed into a harvest of fruit.

Alice Parker approached them; her dress a little less conservative than yesterday's dress, but not so bad it was inappropriate in front of the children the way her usual attire was.

"How nice to see you both," Alice said, her voice dripping with sarcasm. "I see you brought your *wife!*" She held up her fingers to make air quotes and snickered.

Noel smiled and nodded; he liked that the woman couldn't ruffle her feathers; she sure ruffled his!

"I was so excited when I saw you'd changed your mind and entered the bachelor's auction tonight; I'll be your highest bidder!" She walked away after snickering at Noel.

He didn't like that.

Why did she have to do that? There were plenty of single men in town who she could bid on—Jack Baker, for instance.

"I'm so sorry she acts that way; I hope she didn't upset you,"

"I don't mind," she said, betraying her heart. "I know the auction is for charity and it's controlled within the event, so it really isn't a real date—not like *she* thinks."

"That's true," he agreed. "The highest bidder gets to have dinner with me at the pavilion and then a fifteen-minute sleigh ride afterward. When you think of it that way, the bidders don't really get much for their money, and I've seen bids as high as five-hundred dollars!"

He'd forgotten about the bachelor auction, and now he regretted agreeing to it.

NOEL had no idea she was capable of feeling so jealous. Hunter stood on the platform and it was his time to be bid on; what was she going to do? She could see Alice Parker among the crowd of women lined up in front of the platform; the woman had money, and she would outbid Noel's measly twenty-five dollars. That was all she was prepared to bid, and even that was stretching it. She tried to tell herself it was only for charity and that it wouldn't mean anything, but these *English* women were serious. She took a deep breath; she was shaking, and her heart was racing as the auctioneer opened up the bidding for Hunter.

"Let's start the bidding at, shall we say, one hundred dollars?"

Every woman raised her hand; Noel groaned inwardly.

He's too popular; I'm out before I even got started!

Hunter had jokingly offered to let her bid higher and he would pay the bid, but she couldn't let him do that; that was like paying to date *her!* Was that the sign she'd been looking for and she'd missed it? Did he want to date *her?*

The bidding was now up to five-hundred dollars. That was way out of Hunter's budget, she was certain, but what could she do?

Alice Parker held up her hand. "One Thousand Dollars!"

All the other women groaned.

Noel's heart skipped a beat as she watched the look of torment on Hunter's face.

The auctioneer slammed down his gavel. "A Thousand Dollars; do I hear more?"

Silence except for a few more groans.

Alice Parker flashed a look of satisfaction that filled her with a bit of anger.

She had to do something, but what?

"A Thousand Dollars going once, going twice…"

Noel held up her hand. "Free cookies for life!"

Laughter erupted among the gathering crowd.

The mayor stepped up to the podium and whispered something while the auctioneer covered the microphone with his hand.

Once the mayor sat back down, the auctioneer smacked his gavel once more.

"Folks, we have a new bid—an unusual bid, but Mayor Abbott believes it outbids the current bid of a Thousand Dollars."

More laughter from the crowd.

"Do I hear anymore bids?"

Noel's heart felt as if it stopped as she waited for Alice Parker to object, but she didn't.

"Free Cookies for life, going once, going twice—sold! To the young lady with the cookies!"

Hunter stood there smiling at Noel and she couldn't be prouder of herself for thinking of such a tactic at the last minute, especially as nervous as she was.

He jumped down from the stage and pulled her into his arms and twirled her. She couldn't stop laughing until he put her down.

"What made you think of such a thing to bid?" he asked, smiling wider than she'd ever seen him.

She giggled. "You looked like you needed rescuing!"

CHAPTER FOURTEEN

NOEL was still shaking, but felt an exhilaration when the mayor approached her about her winning bid.

"I've never had a bid so clever! My wife brings home your cookies a little too often," he said, patting his belly and laughing. "So, I knew that would be the perfect way to keep our refreshment costs down, but I don't want you to worry that we'll be taking advantage of you; your bakery has been such a blessing to this community."

She smiled. "Thank you, Mr. Mayor."

Hunter shook his hand. "I'll see you in my shop on Monday to pick up that new TV cabinet for your living room."

"I'll be there," he said. "But right now, I'm going to get out of your hair because this young lady paid a pretty steep price for a date with you tonight, and I'm not going to interrupt another minute of it. Now, you let me know if he disappoints you, and I'll have a talk with him!" He winked and smiled.

She laughed. "I have a feeling he won't disappoint me."

He bid them goodnight and left them to their date.

"Do you mind if we all eat together?"

He bowed and smiled. "It's *your* date; you paid for it, so tonight, I'm all yours!"

"I'll send Gabby home with Becca for the sleigh ride; I don't think she's dressed warm enough for that."

"I was planning on having Pop take Raegan home; she'll be worth nothing after I get some dinner in her."

He held out his arm for her. "Let's go have some dinner; I'm so starved I could eat a lifetime supply of your cookies!"

She giggled, and Hunter felt a warming in his heart he hadn't felt in a long time.

With the girls on their way home, Hunter walked through the park with Noel on his arm. Wispy snowflakes and a gentle breeze played with the auburn tendrils at her temples. She continually tucked it back behind her ear, but

Hunter liked it. He'd imagined more than once what her hair would look like if it were pulled down and allowed to flutter around her face. It was beautiful, and it looked so soft he wanted to run his fingers through it.

He glanced at his watch and pointed to the sleigh parked where Noel's buggy was only a few minutes ago. The sleigh had wheels on the bottoms of the runners, so it wasn't an authentic sleigh, but it was as close as they could get in this town. He knew some of the Amish families on the outskirts of town owned sleighs, but he was grateful it wasn't being Amish-driven. She seemed to have separated herself from the Amish in the past couple days, and he was happy that she'd done that for him. The last thing he wanted was to drive her back to the community; he'd rather she continued to move toward his—the *English*.

"I believe we're next," Hunter said.

With eight couples that were matched with bids, it would take the driver a little over two hours to give everyone their ride for the evening, but he'd noticed Alice and her winning bid of Jack Baker leaving to go to the diner across the street.

"I really hope it works out for the two of them," Noel said.

"I think you just want to make sure she isn't going to keep chasing after me!"

"And I thought you wanted the same thing," she said with a chuckle.

He smiled and patted her hand. "Of course, I do; she isn't my type."

"What is your type?"

He stopped short of the sleigh and turned to her. "I like women who smell like gingerbread!"

She giggled. "Is that so? I would have taken you for a bacon sort of guy!"

His head bobbed up and down. "Bacon's good too!"

"Did I tell you I specialize in bacon?" she boasted.

He pushed out his lower lip and nodded. "Good to know."

The driver of the sleigh hollered *next.*

"I believe that's our sleigh ride waiting." Hunter wiped the snow from the seat before he assisted her up into the sleigh. He climbed up beside her and grabbed the wool blankets from under the seat and spread them over their laps.

She snuggled in close to him, and he tucked his arm around her. Snowflakes swirled around them and the jingling of the sleigh bells echoed in the cold night air. They leaned back and looked at the stars that peeked around the clouds when they moved. Having her in his arms made him feel alive again; he noticed life around him again—as if seeing them for the first time.

His head was in a whirlwind until suddenly, and far too soon for his liking, the sleigh stopped. He hated that their *date* was considered officially over, but perhaps he could persuade her to spend a little more time with him. He helped her down from the sleigh after folding the blankets and tucking them back under the seat bench. Then he tipped the driver and tucked her arm back in the crook of his elbow. They walked down the lane under the candy canes; the lights were still on, but nearly everyone had gone home. The band, however, still played. He led her into the center of the park in front of the gazebo and winked at the orchestra leader who conducted the brass instruments.

A slow waltz began to play, and he bowed slightly to Noel. "May I have this dance?"

She giggled and nodded; he pulled her into his arms and twirled her around, the cement pad lightly dusted with snow. It made for a slippery dance, but it almost made it more fun. He didn't ever want to let her go; he had fallen in love with her, and all he wanted to do was kiss her.

Did he dare?

Perhaps he would save that for after he dropped her at her doorstep.

NOEL waited for Hunter to open the heavy door to his truck and assist her. She liked that he was a gentleman, but more than that, she was hoping for another opportunity to be in his arms before they had to say goodnight.

He opened the passenger door and she placed her hands on his shoulders, and when she slid down from the truck, she slid right into his arms. She paused, afraid if she broke eye-contact, it would break the spell between them.

He dipped his head to kiss her, but paused only long enough until she gave him a consenting nod. She would give him her heart freely; she already loved him.

His lips touched hers with a soft warmth and a gentle moan as he deepened the kiss. She sucked in a breath, his aftershave drawing her closer; she wanted to breathe him in, melt into him. It frightened and excited her, causing her whole body to quake in the strength of his arms.

He swept his lips across her mouth, then her cheek, and moved his way to her neck, sending prickles of heat all the way to her toes. She couldn't catch her breath before his lips were consuming hers again. Her eyes fluttered open and closed, his lips on her neck tickled her. He tucked his arm around her and pulled her closer, while his mouth devoured hers once more. Her breath came out in shallow pants as he reached back and unpinned her hair; she was his, and there was no turning back.

CHAPTER FIFTEEN

HUNTER answered his phone with a sleepy voice.

"Little brother, what are you still doing in bed?"

"I had a late night," he said. "Pop is feeding Rae her breakfast and I'm trying to sleep in—at least, I was."

"I haven't heard from you for almost a week and I talk to Pop and he tells me you were out on a date last night!"

"Pop's got a big mouth," Hunter grumbled sleepily.

"So, it wasn't a date?" she asked.

He sighed.

"I knew something was up when you didn't call me back after the cookie thing," she said sucking in a breath. "Oh my gosh! Are you seeing that Amish woman?"

Hunter snored real loudly into the phone, suppressing the urge to laugh.

"I know you're not asleep, little brother; you're avoiding, which means I got it right!"

"Yes, you guessed it; I'll get you an extra ugly sweater for Christmas this year."

"Oh, please don't!" she said. "But do tell me about your date; are things serious between you?"

"I'm going to see Mr. Edwards," he said.

"Oh, Hunter, do you think you'll spook her? It's sort of sudden, don't you think?"

"I thought so at first, but after spending every day with her, I feel like I've known her all my life, and life is too short to waste on *what-ifs*. I don't want to play it safe; I want to live again. Besides, Raegan needs a mom and Gabby—her daughter, needs a dad. We'd be a ready-made family, but if she says yes to my proposal, I'm going to marry her and love her for the rest of my life."

"I'm so happy for you, Hunter, but I'm going to be there the day after Christmas, and I'm dragging Hayden along with me. Don't go off and get married before we get there!"

"Don't worry—I know better!"

He hung up the phone and rolled over, unable to get Noel's kisses off his mind. He'd set up in advance to have the city band play for them under the stars, hoping it would create a perfect setting for them.

First, he had to go see the jeweler and start things off right. He'd promised in front of Jack Baker that he would get her a ring, and he prayed she would like it.

NOEL took one last look in the mirror at her long hair she'd left down for the man she hoped would soon be her husband. She'd carefully picked out a conservative *English* dress in a deep green velvet with a white lace collar and a red bow at the waist. It was her first Christmas dress, and one she hoped to make memories in. Hunter had made a fuss about their date tonight; she was giddy like a young girl waiting for her first kiss. She hoped that every kiss they shared would be as special as their first.

Hunter walked into the bakery; she'd already sent Becca and Gabby over to his place to spend the evening with Raegan.

Her breath hitched when their eyes met; his long black coat covered a charcoal pinstripe suit, the royal blue dress shirt matched his eyes. He'd slicked back his dark brown hair, the ends flipping up just past his ears. The scruff on his jawline blended with his goatee, but his upper lip was clean-shaven. He was handsome, and his manly scent stole her breath away, making her dizzy with love for him.

Her heart thumped when he closed the space between them, her lips begging to be kissed. The warmth of his touch melted her as he pulled her into his arms. His fingers swept through her hair, causing prickles to radiate around her scalp.

"I had this whole thing planned, but I can't wait another minute," he whispered in her ear, breathing out and causing tingles of desire to trickle down her spine. "I don't want to be fancy with you, I want things to be simple for us—plain, the way you're used to."

I don't mind the fancy stuff!

He released her and bent on one knee before her and pulled out a little black box from his lapel pocket. He opened it and held it up for her to see.

She gasped, tears welled up in her eyes.

"I love you, Noel; I don't know how or when it happened, but I feel as if somehow I've always loved you. I want to make you and Gabby part of my family; will you do me the honor of becoming my wife?"

"*Jah*—yes!" she said. "I love you too, Hunter; I always have."

He rose from bended knee and kissed her gently at first, but then with the passion of a man who loved her more than he could possibly express.

She giggled as she fanned her fingers to admire the ring. "I never thought I would want a ring on my finger for marriage—it isn't allowed—if you're Amish. It's considered a sign of vanity, but I know that among the *English,* it's a symbol of your love and commitment. So, for that reason, I will wear this ring and be proud to be your wife."

He smiled. "You've made me so happy."

"I know two little girls who are going to be happy about it too," she said.

"Would you like to have our special date now?" he asked. "I suppose now we really have something to celebrate!"

He helped her into her coat and she wrapped a long, knit scarf around her head and grabbed her gloves.

"Do you mind walking?"

She chuckled nervously. "That depends on how far we're going."

"Just across the street to the park; the mayor did me a little favor."

"How much did his little *favor* cost you?"

"One TV cabinet at half-price, but it was worth it!"

She giggled and tucked her hand in his as he led her across the street to the park.

They walked to the center of the park, the band playing another waltz, and though the night was clear, a snow-making machine sent snowflakes fluttering down inside the gazebo and over the makeshift dance floor.

He pulled her into a dance and kissed her under the stars, as she admired the sparkly diamond ring on her finger.

When the dance was finished, he bowed. "Would you like to have dinner with me?"

"Of course, I would."

Inside the pavilion, a table for two was set with gold-rimmed china plates, with a red tablecloth and a small topiary tree in the center with holly berries and a red bow around the base of the planter. Crystal water glasses and stainless silverware folded into cream-colored napkins were centered on the top of each plate. Overhead, in the rafters, small twinkly, white lights filled the pavilion with a soft, warm glow. It was like a fancy wedding.

She giggled. "You did all this for me?"

He pushed back a stray curl from her cheek and kissed her gently, a mischievous smile tugging at the corners of his mouth. "You do owe the city free cookies for life because of me; the least I can do is be there to help you bake them!"

THE END

LOOK for Book 2 in this series…

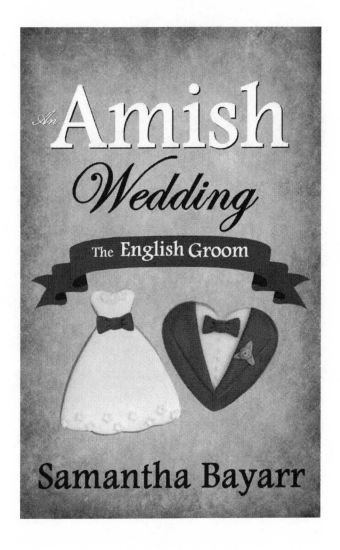

An Amish Wedding

The English Groom

Samantha Bayarr

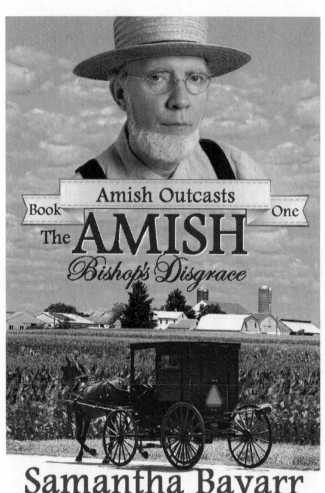

Amish Outcasts

Book One

The **AMISH**

Bishop's Disgrace

Samantha Bayarr

Amish Romance Suspense

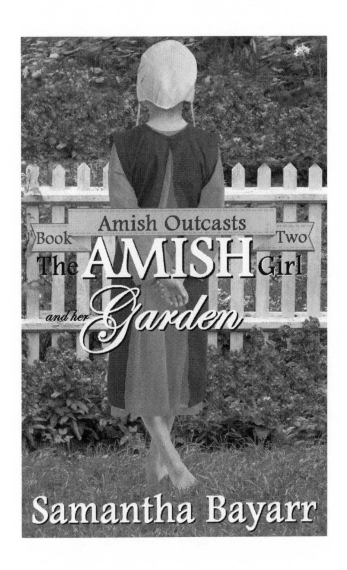

Amish Outcasts

Book Two

The AMISH Girl and her Garden

Samantha Bayarr

Newly Released books
99 cents or FREE with
Kindle Unlimited.

♡ LOVE to Read?
♡ LOVE 99 cent Books?
♡ LOVE GIVEAWAYS?

SIGN UP NOW
Click the Link Below to Join
my Exclusive Mailing List

PLEASE CLICK <u>HERE</u> to SIGN UP!

Made in the USA
Middletown, DE
08 December 2017